SAMANTHA JACOBS

Misty Hilll

Cursed Asylum

This book is dedicated to my mom, Cheryl Scheepers, my very first reader, and number one fan.
Thank you for always supporting me in my dream, and even getting involved with ideas for my books.

Acknowledgement

Cheryl Scheepers - My amazing mom and number one fan. Without you, this book would not have been possible.

Pru - A fellow author and my best friend who is always willing to listen to my ideas and read my works.

1

Chapter 1

"Misty Meadows? You've got to be kidding me."

"You get on the bus in an hour, you'll arrive around eight."

"I can't believe this. You can't seriously want to send me to that crappy place."

"Kane, there are no other options; she's your only guardian."

Kane London.

Alice Gomes sighed, Kane was her granddaughter, but she had never met the girl.

Alice's daughter and son-in-law had died two months ago in a car crash, and Alice had been left as the girl's guardian.

The social worker had sent Alice a thick file on every detail of the girl, and when Alice had gone through it, she hadn't been entirely thrilled at the idea of taking Kane in.

She had been kicked out of several schools for fighting.

She had a criminal record for assault and carrying weapons.

Alice feared she would cause havoc in the little town of Misty Meadows, however, she was family and Alice couldn't turn her back on blood.

Black combat boots hit the dusty road as Kane jumped off the bus.

She looked around an empty dirt road, her bag on her shoulder.

It was only half-past eight, but everything looked dead as if there was no life in the town.

As the bus drove away, Kane turned to see a very poor excuse for a shop.

She went into the shop, stopping at the counter, "Hey, you don't happen to know an old woman by the name of Alice Gomes, do you?"

The skinny guy behind the counter looked up through his large glasses, "Yes! Mrs. Gomes is a really lovely lady."

Kane frowned, "Mind telling me where to find her?"

"Oh, I can't give those details-"

"Dude, stop smiling, your braces are blinding me. I'm a relative of the old bat."

He didn't seem too pleased with the reply, "Could you leave?"

Kane rolled her eyes. "Happily." She walked out, sneaking a chocolate bar into her pocket on the way.

Opening the chocolate, she took a bite and took her phone from her pocket, dialing her best friend from back home.

"Kane?! Hey, how's it going?"

"Dead. Listen, what did that social worker bitch say I must do when I get here?"

"Go to your gran without getting into trouble. Oh, and don't get arrested."

"Ah, but what were the directions?"

"I can't remember, K."

Kane grinned, getting an idea, "Never mind, I'll get her to come to me."

Hanging up, she returned to the store, grabbing a packet of crisps, she headed back towards the door.

The nerd behind the counter jumped to his feet, "You can't just take that, you have to pay."

Kane grinned, "Why don't you call the cops?"

He frowned, "For a bag of chips?"

Kane rolled her eyes and kicked a shelf over before walking out and sitting down, opening the bag and listened to brace-face call the cops.

"That idiot wouldn't give me your details." She sat explaining to Alice, who had been called to the police station and had picked her up and taken her home.

Alice frowned, "You could have found another way to get to me. What you did was uncalled for."

Kane rolled her eyes, "Yeah, yeah, blah, blah, blah, got you. Where's my room?"

Alice sighed, "Follow me. And we will finish this conversation tomorrow."

She followed Alice to a small room, painted light blue; the covers were white with pink flowers.

"Well, this is disgusting."

Alice sighed, "Goodnight, Kane."

Kane closed the door and dropped her bag onto the small desk in the room.

Going over to the bed, she looked out of the window, into the backyard, which was rather close to a woodsy area, a very dark area.

Kane frowned, suddenly getting the feeling that there was someone out there watching her.

Sighing, she closed the curtains, trying to tell herself that she was imagining it suddenly the curtains swung open, and there stood a man in between the trees.

"Alice!"

But by the time Alice came in, he was gone.

"A man was standing there."

Alice frowned, "It's a new place, don't worry yourself. Get some sleep." She closed the curtains and walked out.

The next morning Kane had a shower before Alice dropped her at school.

Kane went to her first class, the teacher introduced her to the class, there was a girl who gave her dirty looks, then again, the whole class was giving her dirty looks, it was probably her attire which consisted of ripped black jeans, black combat boots and a black tank top with a red and black plaid shirt hanging loosely over it.

She made it to lunchtime without punching anyone, which she thought was a pretty big achievement.

Taking a seat at an empty table, she thought she had found some peace.

Suddenly the brace face from the store sat down opposite her, "Hey, how do you like school?"

"Go away, brace face."

"It's Cliff. Cliff Olsen."

"Like I care."

He raised his brows, "I'm the only one being nice to you."

Kane shrugged, "I don't recall asking anyone to be nice."

He sighed but didn't move.

Kane looked over at the 'popular' table, "Who are they?"

"Veda Matthews; voted best looking female student for three years in a row, she's the Queen Bee here. Her boyfriend, Brent Hartley, voted best looking male student last year. The blond is Layla King, she's Veda's best friend, also in second place for best looking female student. The guy next to her is Jack Brookes, captain of the football team. The girl with the black hair is Cassie Smith, no idea why she hangs out with them because she's nice. The girl with the blond streaks is also really nice, Stacey White. The guy next to her is her boyfriend, Mac West." He stopped and waved to a girl and guy, both with mousy brown hair, who started coming towards them.

Kane frowned, "Why are they coming towards us?"

"They're friends of mine."

Kane raised her brows, "I'm amazed you have any friends."

The two sat down, both smiling at Kane.

The girl smiled, "Hi, I'm Macy, this is Collin."

Kane frowned at the three in front of her, how did I end up with these geeks?

Brace face grinned, "She's Kane."

Macy tilted her head, "Nice name."

"Uh-huh. So, Brace face who's the dude in the corner?" Kane was referring to a guy in the corner of the room, sitting at an empty table, wearing all black, dark bluish-black hair that was passed shoulder length with flame-colored streaks in it.

"Moth. Don't know his real name, and his surname is Star. He's always been weird; he's pretty much an outcast, a loner. No one wants to be around him. He got the name Moth because he was obsessed with flames. Always has a lighter with him."

Kane raised a brow, "How come you lot haven't taken him in? Don't the outcasts normally stick together?"

Collin scoffed, "He's a whole different type of outcast. There was a fire upon Misty Hill that killed and injured a lot of people; everyone says he had something to do with it. Trouble follows him everywhere. It's safer to stay away from him."

Kane was still watching Moth when suddenly he looked up

and their eyes met.

Slowly, he stood and walked out of the room.

"So he's such a freak, that the freaks don't want to be near him?" She asked.

Brace face nodded, "Basically. And we're all kind of scared of him. He's known to have some serious anger issues."

The rest of the day went by and Kane didn't see Moth again.

After school Brace Face walked halfway home with her and then went to start his shift at the store.

Kane didn't go home, she decided to explore the town a bit.

Following an old railroad track, she found a few run down wooden cabins next to a small stream.

"This town is so lame." Crouching, she reached out to run her hand in the water, but the water suddenly went from crystal blue to thick red blood.

She gasped and fell back, landing hard on the ground, frowning when she realized the water was clear again.

"Great, now you're seeing things that aren't there. Again." She got to her feet with a frown on her face, "And having a full-blown conversation with yourself. What next?"

Shaking her head, she decided to go home.

When she got home, she found Alice on the front porch with food set out on the small table.

Kane sat down opposite her, "Any reason we're outside?"

"Fresh air. Why are you late?"

Kane frowned, "I went for a walk."

Alice's eyes flashed, "Where?"

Kane shrugged, "Some old railroad tracks that lead to a stream." With creepy water.

"Well, just don't go walking too far."

Kane was about to reply when she noticed the neighbors,

"Who stays there?"

"The Hartley's, why do you ask?"

"I recognize the one guy from school," she got to her feet and went over to the fence, "Hey, Brent, right?"

He turned and smiled, "Yeah. Kane, right?"

She nodded.

"You stay with Mrs. Gomes?"

Kane nodded, "Yeah. She's my Gran."

"Great, she has dinner with us sometimes. You're welcome to join her at the next one."

She nodded, "Sounds like a plan. I'll see you at school tomorrow." She turned and went back to join Alice.

Alice smiled, "I'm glad to see you making friends."

Kane shrugged, "Not really. His girlfriend and I don't like each other much."

"Yes, Veda does tend to be a bit moody."

Kane stood, "I'm not feeling so good, I'm going to get some sleep."

She went into her room and froze; the guy was between the trees again.

"Alice!"

Alice came rushing in, "What is it?"

Kane turned back to the window, "There he is!"

Alice frowned, "Who?"

Kane frowned, "He's gone again. When I walked in he was standing right there."

Alice closed the curtains, "Just get some sleep."

Alice left, closing the door behind her and Kane walked slowly over to the bed.

First, the guy disappearing last night, then the stream changing, and now this again.

"What is going on?"

You're going crazy. Again.

Kane shook her head, hoping she would feel better after some sleep.

The next morning when Kane got to school, Brent greeted her, leaving Veda fuming.

Kane made it through the first half of the day without any problems.

When she got to the lunchroom, Brent waved, motioned for her to join them.

But what she noticed was Veda, Layla and Jack, who stood in front of Brace Face, Macy sitting at the table looking nervous.

Kane narrowed her eyes and walked up to them, "Veda, what are you doing?"

Veda turned and smiled, "Just having some fun with Brace Face over here."

Kane noticed that his glasses were askew and he flinched when Jack went to pat him on the shoulder before he left with Layla and Veda.

Brace Face sighed and sat down next to Macy.

Kane put her tray down, "Okay, so what happened?"

Macy sighed, "They tend to rough Cliff up from time to–"

Kane didn't hear the rest of what Macy was saying because she was already at Veda's table.

She slammed her tray down, "You people need to start learning some things."

Veda eyed her suspiciously, "Excuse me?"

"What the hell gives you the right to pick on Bra–Cliff? You are a bunch of cowards for picking on someone who can't fight back. Not to mention that there were three of you."

Veda rolled her eyes, "I'll keep that in mind the next time I want to please you."

Kane clenched her teeth, 'Don't start a fight.'

"White trash."

Too late. Kane lent over the table, grabbed the empty tray in front of Brent, swinging it straight into Jack's face, knocking him off his chair.

Layla jumped onto the table, trying to kick Kane in the face, but Kane grabbed her ankle and pulled, sending Layla crashing down.

Veda got to her feet, trying to run; Kane grabbed a fistful of her hair and smashed her face into the table.

She looked up and frowned, the whole room was watching her.

Moth included.

And that's when the principal walked in.

"Kane London, my office. Now!"

He turned and stormed out, with a sigh, Kane followed.

Once in his office, he sat down at his desk, "Miss London, I have seen your previous track record. Kicked out of seven schools. In jail for assault, carrying unlicensed weapons, and fraud."

Kane grinned, "And I'm not even twenty yet."

He frowned, "It's nothing to brag about Miss London. You can't come to my school and start fights-"

Kane cut him off, "Whoa! Hold up a second. Veda, Layla and Jack were harassing Cliff. When I asked, rather nicely if they would leave him alone, I was called white trash. Doesn't even make sense when she's white herself."

"It still doesn't mean that fighting is okay."

Kane stood, "Screw this. If you're going to expel me, do it."

He sighed, "Detention for a month after school."

Kane walked out, making sure to slam the door hard.

As soon as she was back in the hall, she kicked over one of the bins.

"Anger issues much?"

She turned, "Brent? Hey."

"Mr. Lewis give you any trouble?"

Kane shrugged, "A month detention after school."

"Ouch."

Kane laughed, "Not really, I've dealt with a lot worse."

Brent frowned, "Like?"

"Story for another day."

"Well, this might make you feel better. I've just come from the nurse; Veda's going to have some bad bruising."

Kane laughed, "Well, she better stay away from me, or she'll have a lot worse."

After detention Kane was on her way home when she noticed a small path, leading up a hill.

Kane frowned, "You know you shouldn't go up there."

She stood still for a total of five seconds before following the path.

It came to a stop at a very old, shell of a house.

The house had been a small place, and it had obviously burnt down.

The few walls that still stood were burnt black, the roof and door gone.

"This must be Misty Hill."

She went into the house, stepping around the debris.

The place was dark and the sun had set almost at the same moment she had stepped into the house.

She took a step forward and a hand snaked around her mouth,

another around her waist.

She struggled before elbowing the person in the ribs and running.

She made it halfway to the pathway when someone tackled her, landing on top of her.

She turned on her back to see Moth.

"Moth?!"

He froze, "What are you doing here?" "I went for a walk, what- could you get the hell off me- are you doing here?"

He got to his feet and helped her up, "I, uh, kind of stay here."

Kane frowned, "Is this the place they say you burned down?"

He clenched his jaw, "You should leave."

Kane rolled her eyes, "Jeez, talk about rude."

"No one comes up here. You shouldn't either."

"I can go wherever I want to."

"Misty Meadows isn't the safest of places."

Kane scoffed, "Neither is jail."

"What was that?"

Kane shook her head, "Nothing. I better get going."

She turned and took to the path; she was halfway down when she realized that Moth was following her.

She frowned, "What are you doing?"

"Walking you home." He replied as if it was obvious.

"I can do that myself just fine."

"I didn't say that you couldn't."

"Then stop."

"I am not having you go missing when the last place you were seen was up there. I don't need to be blamed for another murder."

Kane kept her mouth firmly shut for once.

"Where do you stay?" he asked.

"Alice Gomes."

He seemed to slow his stride slightly, "You're family?"

"You sure are nosy."

"Just making conversation."

Kane had a feeling there was more to it than that.

Moth stopped in front of Alice's yard.

Kane frowned, "You know where it is?"

"Everyone knows her." He turned and walked away.

Kane walked in and dropped her bag at the door.

"Why are you late this time?"

"Detention."

Alice stood, "It's your second day and you're already getting into trouble. What did you do?"

Kane sighed, "Beat up some kids for picking on Cliff and calling me trash."

"You can't go hitting people, Kane! I don't know how my daughter raised you but–"

Kane cut her off, "Whoa, I don't care who you are, you do not get to speak about my mother."

Alice sighed, "Kane, you need to stop being so violent. And you also need to start realizing that you have to follow rules, whether you like it or not."

Kane shrugged, "I don't have to do anything." She pushed passed Alice and went into her room.

The next day Veda and Layla weren't at school.

Jack was, with bruising on his face.

At lunch, she went to her usual table where Cliff, Collin and Macy already sat waiting.

She couldn't help but notice that Moth was nowhere in sight.

Collin grinned, "I hear you put on a good show yesterday."

Kane shrugged as she sat down, "It was nothing."

Macy chewed on her lip, "Well now the whole school is more scared of you than Veda."

Kane looked at her blankly, "So?"

"You can take her place." Said Cliff.

Macy nodded, "Yeah, you don't have to sit with us anymore."

Kane rolled her eyes, "I don't want to be liked. I just wanted to let them know not to mess with me."

Collin smiled, "At least they'll leave us alone now."

"And if they don't, you tell me." Said Kane.

Cliff shook his head, "No, you don't need any more trouble."

Kane glared at him, "You tell me, or I'll be the one beating the crap out of you."

The three nodded.

Kane turned, scanning the room for Moth; he was still nowhere in sight.

The bell rang and when they walked out of the lunchroom, Brent stopped them.

"Hey, Kane?"

"What?"

"I couldn't help noticing you came home really late last night."

Kane frowned, "Yeah, so?"

He raised a brow, "I also saw who you were with."

Kane scoffed, "And? The last time I checked, who I walk with has nothing to do with you."

Brent let out a humorless laugh, "You're kidding, right? Hanging out with the geeks that I can still understand. But hanging around with a killer? That's a bit much."

"Now you can match your pathetic girlfriend." her fist connected with his face.

"Kane London, my office."

Kane sighed; she hadn't realized Mr. Lewis had been right there.

Shaking her head, she followed him.

Closing the door behind her, she sat on his desk and smiled, "What's up, Lewis?"

"It's Mr. Lewis. Look, I'm trying my best to help you, but you're not making it very easy."

"I don't want or need your help."

He sighed, "I know your grandmother very well, and we've been friends since we were in school. I watched your mother grow up. Don't go the same way she-"

Kane stood, "The same way? Are you trying to say something?"

"Not at all. I'm only saying that she was a very good girl, straight A student. But all of that changed and she became very rebellious-"

And at that exact moment Kane's fist connected with his nose, sending him flying backwards and off his chair.

"When are people going to learn to shut their mouths about my mother? I know all about her life and I do not need anyone filling me in!" she turned and stormed out.

"Kane? Are you okay?" Asked Cliff as she passed him.

She held up thumbs up as she walked out of the school doors.

She walked for a while before spotting an unfinished building, going up the breaking stairs to the roof.

She sat down, making herself comfortable.

She planned to stay for a while, Lewis would have told Alice by now and she wasn't in the mood for that.

Closing her eyes, she decided to try and get some rest.

"Hey, wake up."

Kane opened her eyes to see Moth nudging her.

The first thing she noticed was that the sun was gone and the full moon was in its place.

Kane frowned, "What are you doing here?"

"I was going to ask you the same question. You do realize it's not safe up here, right?"

Kane stood, "Oh please."

"Really, it's not. The place could collapse at any second. And any crazy person could decide to come up here."

Kane rolled her eyes, "This town is so small it probably doesn't even have anyone crazy."

Moth sighed, "You'd be surprised."

Kane shrugged, "Maybe I would."

"Well, either way, you need to stop walking around at night."

"Why? Don't want to be accused of more murders?"

He clenched his jaw, "Something like that."

He turned his back on her, taking a Zippo from his pocket and flicking it on and off.

Kane frowned, "That probably doesn't help those rumors about the fire."

He kept toying with the lighter.

"Probably doesn't help that you sleep in that old–"

He spun, "Don't you dare mention that to anyone."

Kane took a step back, "Why? Got something to hide?"

He glared at her, "Don't push me, London."

Kane narrowed her eyes, "Or what? You'll set me alight?"

He clenched his jaw and took a step forward.

Kane misjudged and took a step back, her foot off the roof, swaying, she went backwards.

Moth grabbed her and pulled her back.

"What the hell is wrong with you? You could have died! And the screwed up thing is that everyone would have blamed me."

"Don't take it out on me because you're the town freak."

"You don't even know what happened!"

Kane pushed past him and went down the stairs, she was in the road already when he caught up with her.

"What did I tell you about walking around at night?"

Kane ignored him.

"You wanna get yourself killed? Fine, just don't do it when I'm the last person you were with."

Kane sighed, "It's not like I want to be around you."

"Then do a better job of staying away from me!"

"Really? Do you honestly think I want to be around a pyromaniac?"

"You don't know a thing about me, yet you think you have the right to judge me? Who the hell do you think you are, London?"

Kane frowned, "It's not about who I think I am, it's about who I know I am, you idiot!"

"And who is that? A crazy girl who starts fights in school and thinks she better than everyone?"

"Well, at least I'm not accused of being a killer!"

He glared at her before storming off.

Kane stormed into Alice's house and slammed the door.

Alice glared at her, "You punched another student and the principal. And you're late again. And what were you doing with that Star boy?"

Kane sighed, "Lewis was talking about my mother. I like being outside at night. And as for the other student, Brent asked for it."

"You ignored my last question, Kane.'

Kane shrugged.

Alice frowned, "You are not to be around him. He's trouble."

Kane scoffed, "Like I'm not."

"Just stay away from him, Kane."
"I can be friends with whoever I want.'
She walked away from Alice, going into her room.

2

Chapter 2

The next morning Kane left the house before Alice was up.

she went to the store where Cliff worked.

She slammed her hand on the counter, "Hey, Brace-Face, shifts up."

He frowned, "What?"

"I'm bored. You wont miss any customers, the place has less life than a funeral home," she frowned, "Where's the rest of the geek squad?"

Cliff shrugged, "Not sure."

She sighed, "where does Moth go on a weekend?"

Cliff frowned, "Why?"

Kane, "Curious."

He sighed, "He's dangerous."

"Who?"

"Moth." Replied Cliff.

Macy's mouth dropped, "Kane!"

Kane held up her hands, "I was just asking."

And in walked Brent.

He stopped, "Kane, we good?"

She nodded.

"Good, I want to apologize to all of you for what I said."

Macy smiled, "No problem. I'm sure Kane would also like to apologize."

Kane scoffed, "No, Kane does not. I don't do shit I need to apologize to. I never apologize. You deserved it."

Brent sighed.

"I'll see you guys later." She walked out, going to the path and up to Misty Hill.

"Moth?"

Silence.

Kane walked into the burnt down house.

She found a room with a mattress and a few other things in it.

Continuing, she found a smaller room and bent to examine the wall, it had a thin stain of blood on it.

She stood and froze; there was a mirror on the wall.

But it wasn't the mirror that made her blood run cold; it was what stared back at her from inside the mirror.

It wasn't her reflection, it was a charred female face, the bottom half of the face with no skin.

Kane screamed and ran out, running down the pathway, by the time she got to the bottom, she wished she hadn't worn shorts, her legs were covered in small cuts and scrapes from the branches in the path.

She let out a stressed sigh and started walking, seeing a mechanics shop, she stopped.

There was Moth.

He was packing tools into boxes.

"Moth."

He looked up, surprised to see her, "What?"

Kane shrugged, "I'm, uh, sorry. For what I said last night."

He went back to packing.

"I'm apologizing, you idiot."

He didn't bother looking up, "I don't care."

"Okay, then. What are you doing?"

"You never saw anyone pack before?"

Kane crossed her arms, "Why are you packing?"

"moving shop," he looked up and frowned, "What happened to you?"

"I fell."

"Where?"

"None of your business."

He looked as if he wanted to say something but thought better of it.

Kane looked around, "Weekend job?"

"Full time."

"What about school?"

He shrugged, "I left."

She frowned, "You're not going to be around anymore?"

He stopped and looked up, "Why?"

She shrugged, "Just wondering if I'll still be seeing you around."

"Don't."

Kane frowned, "What?"

Moth sighed, "Don't concern yourself with me."

Kane laughed, "it wasn't concern."

Moth smirked before resuming his packing, "Keep telling yourself that."

"I thought I'd find you here."

Kane turned to see Collin and Macy with Brent close behind.

Moth glanced at Brent, "Nice eye makeup. It suits you."

"Freak show. Your mother knew to get away from you; 'like

father like son'.'"

Moth jumped to his feet, heading straight for Brent.

Kane grabbed him by the arm, "Moth."

He stopped, not taking his eyes from Brent, "Get your hand off me, London."

"No, he's trying to get a reaction."

"Well, it worked.'

Kane tightened her grip on him, "Moth."

He sighed, "Fine." He turned away.

Macy tilted her head, "Kane, you want to come with us? We're waiting for Cliff to finish his shift."

Kane turned to Brent, "you're hanging out with the nerds now?'

He shrugged.

Kane smirked, "Careful there, you might stop being so popular."

He laughed, "As if."

Kane turned back to Macy, "You go ahead. I'll catch up."

"You sure?" No one missed the look on Macy's face.

Kane nodded, "I'm sure."

The three walked away slowly.

Kane turned to Moth, "What the hell was that about?"

Moth sighed, "Stop trying to be my friend, London."

Kane frowned, "I'm not trying to be your anything." She walked out.

Moth watched as she walked away and shook his head, "You're an idiot, Moth."

Frowning, he threw the box across the room.

×

"You can't sit there, Kane."

Kane frowned, "Says who?"

"My boss."

Kane shrugged.

Brent gave her an amused smile, "You love trouble, don't you?"

"Trouble loves me."

The sheriff walked in.

Kane recognized him from her first night in Misty Meadows when she was arrested.

She grinned, "What's up, Sheriff, can't stay away?"

He sighed, "I'm looking for Moth."

Kane spoke before anyone else had the chance, "Why?"

"I'm afraid that's confidential." He replied.

Kane raised a brow, "Then I'm afraid we can't help you."

The sheriff turned, "Cliff?"

He shrugged, "I've been working all day, haven't taken much notice of Moth."

The sheriff turned to the other three, "Any of you know where he is?"

Collin shrugged, "Macy and I have been here with Cliff the whole time."

He turned to Brent, "Don't even think about lying to me."

Brent sighed, "Uncle Rick, c'mon, tell us what's up. We'll keep it to ourselves."

Rick sighed, "Someone's gone missing. We need to question Moth."

Kane frowned, "Whoa, so automatically he gets questioned?"

"Kane, right? I'm just doing my job."

"Not very well."

And then Moth walked in, freezing when he saw Rick.

Rick smiled, "Just the person I was looking for."

"What did I do this time?"

Rick crossed his arms, "Where were you this morning?"

"At the workshop, packing."

"Really? And someone can verify that?"

"I was there with him, the whole time." Lied Kane.

Moth looked at her, but she kept her eyes on Rick.

Rick narrowed his eyes at her, "Really?"

Moth jumped in, "We were packing up for the move. London knew about it, so she offered to help. We were busy till about ten minutes ago."

Rick frowned, "I'll be watching both of you." He walked out.

Macy exhaled loudly, "What the hell, Kane?"

Brent shook his head, "Yeah, I don't get why you did that."

Moth frowned at her, "You shouldn't have done that, you've associated yourself with me."

"Not to mention, you lied to a cop." Added Collin.

Kane shrugged, "Come on, we all know he would have found some way to pin it on Moth."

Brent cleared his throat, "Is this a good time to point out that we don't know if he's guilty or not?"

Moth and Kane glared at him.

Cliff sighed, "What's done is done. Let's leave it at that."

Moth turned back to Kane, "You shouldn't have done that, but thank you."

"Don't mention it."

Moth walked to the back, picked up a juice, returning to the counter, he stood awkwardly in front of Kane, who still sat on the counter.

She took the juice from his hands and passed it to Cliff.

After paying, Moth all but ran out of the store.

Macy shook her head, "Kane, seriously, don't go there."

Kane rolled her eyes, "I'm not going anywhere. I just don't

like to see people falsely accused."

"So create an alibi. What if he's guilty?" Asked Brent.

Kane shrugged.

Brent sighed, shaking his head, "I can't believe you-"

Cliff cut him off, "It's her choice to stand up for him! Get over it or get out."

Kane smiled, "Nicely done, Cliff."

Brent sighed, "I just don't want you to get yourself into any trouble."

"I can handle myself."

But the truth was, she had no idea what she was doing.

After spending the rest of the day with her friends Kane had gone back to the old unfinished buildings roof.

As she stood on the roof, looking out over the town, she wondered about the disappearance, and how Moth had told her it wasn't safe to be out at night.

"Hey."

Kane jumped, spinning to see Moth, "Jeez, Moth, you gave me a fright."

He laughed, "Do you have a death wish or something?"

She was momentarily quiet; it was strange to see Moth laugh.

She shrugged, "I like it outside."

"You've got a yard."

She shrugged, "It's not the same."

He nodded.

"So, uh, have you seen the lightning bugs?" he asked.

She shook her head, "No."

He smiled, "Follow me."

She frowned but followed him; she realized he had led her to the stream.

There were hundreds of tiny lights in the trees.

"It looks amazing."

He nodded, "It's a great place to come if you need to think. But don't, it's not safe."

She laughed, "If it's not safe, why are we here?"

"It's not safe if you're alone."

Kane frowned, "What's wrong with this place? I've heard the stories of how haunted and evil it is."

Moth sighed, getting a faraway look in his eyes, "A lot of people have died here."

"What was Brent talking about when he said your mom left, and the like father, like son thing?"

Moth shook his head, "Let's not go there, London."

Kane sighed, "My parents were killed in a car crash two months ago. They were on their way to fetch me; I had just gotten out of a six-month stay in a mental hospital. They put me in, thinking I was crazy because I was seeing things that no one else could see. Hearing things."

Moth cleared his throat, "My mother didn't leave. My father killed her, but no one knows that. What they do know is that he killed someone, and got off because he swore it was self-defense."

"Where is he?"

"Dead, died in that fire on Misty Hill."

"I'm sorry."

"Don't be, he's where he belongs."

"Moth-"

He cut her off, "Why do you insist on being nice to me?"

"Because where everyone else sees bad, I can see the good."

He frowned, "You shouldn't. And you should listen to everyone and just stay away from me."

She shrugged, "Well, I've never been very good at listening."

He sighed, "Let's get you home."

When Kane walked in, she had a smile on her face.

This vanished when she saw Alice.

"What did I tell you about being with that boy?"

"He's really not a bad person. He walks me home so nothing happens to me."

"He's trouble, Kane."

Kane walked away, going into her room.

Alice followed, "You are not to see him again."

Kane ignored her and started going through her CDs.

"Did you hear me?"

Kane didn't bother looking up, "I'm pretty sure the whole of Misty Meadows heard you."

"Don't give me attitude, Kane; I'm looking out for you."

"I don't need you looking out for me."

"He's a killer."

Kane spun, "What is it with everyone is this town? Must you blame him for everything?"

Alice sighed, "I'm sending you to anger management classes. And if you continue seeing Moth, I'm sending you to a boarding school."

Kane stormed out, leaving Alice calling for her at the door.

It was only when she had lost sight of the house that she realized it was dark, and she had no idea where she was going.

She was going in a direction she had yet to go.

After about fifteen minutes of walking, she found herself in front of the police station.

She stopped, she could hear a man and woman arguing from inside.

Going over to one of the windows, her mouth dropped, it

was Veda and Rick, they were arguing about what was going on between them.

Veda was cheating on Brent with Rick.

Grabbing her phone from her pocket, she hit record.

Once she had enough evidence, she stopped recording and walked away.

The next morning she was walking out the house when her phone rang, she glanced at it before answering; it was her friend from home.

"Hey, Gina."

"Hi, how's Misty Meadows going?"

"It's okay."

"Great, because Scott and I are coming to visit."

Kane frowned, "Scott?"

Silence.

"Gina."

"I'll explain when I see you." And she hung up.

Kane exhaled, Scott was her ex, and by the sounds of it, her friend's current.

Sighing she took a slow walk to the store.

"Hey, Cliff."

He looked up, "Why do you look like you want to kill someone?"

"Long story."

Macy walked in, "Hey, oh God, Kane, why do you look so emo?"

Kane looked down at her dark attire before looking at Macy, who was dressed in a white and pink floral dress.

"I like my look."

Brent walked in, "Where are the other geeks?"

Kane lent over and hit him on the back of the head, "Be nice."

"Collin will join us later." Said, Macy.

Kane frowned, trying to decide if now was a good time to tell him about Rick and Veda.

Brent sighed, "So, another missing person, what's the bet Moth has no alibi?"

Kane rolled her eyes, Nope, he deserves to be humiliated.

"Don't roll your eyes, it's true."

Kane raised a brow, "Do you have an alibi?"

His mouth opened and closed a few times before anything came out, "What the hell, how could you think I'd do something like that?"

"Just pointing out that just because you don't have an alibi, doesn't mean you're guilty."

Macy shrugged, "She's got a point."

"But it's Moth."

Kane frowned, "Why does everyone hate him?"

"Because he's dangerous, he has anger issues and can't be trusted." Replied Brent.

"Glad to see you think so highly of me, Hartley." Said Moth as he walked in.

Kane shrugged, "He's just pointing out that small minds often go with big mouths."

Moth grinned, "Got a point there."

Cliff cleared his throat, "So when did the other person go missing?"

Brent glared at him.

Kane nodded, "Yeah, we need to know, Moth needs an alibi."

Moth frowned, "Not from you, London."

"You got a problem with it coming from me?"

"Actually, yes I do."

Brent snorted, "Talk about gratitude."

Moth glared at him, "Gratitude won't do her any good when she's sitting in a cell."

Kane rolled her eyes, "I don't plan on sitting in a cell.'

"Then stop lying for me."

"Then maybe you should start being smart enough to have a real alibi."

"Why do you even care?"

"I don't."

Moth raised his eyebrows, "It sure looks like you do."

Kane shook her head, "You know what, you're on your own from now on."

He frowned slightly before walking out.

Collin walked in, "Moth was here?"

Kane nodded, "Yeah, how'd you know?"

"He looks rather pissed off; I've noticed you're responsible for that these days."

Kane was on her way home when something caught her eye; it was something running up Misty Hill.

'Don't go chasing after things.'

A second later, she was racing up the hill; freezing when she reached the top and stood in front of the house.

She had not been planning on coming up here again, after seeing the charred face.

Turning, to retreat down the path; her eyes stopping on a wet patch on one of the leaves.

It looked an awful lot like blood.

Just as she was about to reach for the patch, a blood-curdling scream cut through the air; spinning, she ran in the direction in which it had come from, only briefly registering the dark shadow in the burnt house.

Her running was cut short when she caught her jeans on an old piece of barbed wire fencing; trying to rip herself free, she glanced up to see a person jogging towards her from the house, it was dark and the person had a hood on, so she couldn't see their face.

Ripping her jeans free from the fencing, and slicing open her ankle in the process, she continued running in the opposite direction.

Her priority was no longer finding who the scream had belonged to; it was now getting away from the hooded figure.

She had nowhere else to run to when she met with a sheer drop; pausing to take in her surroundings, she saw an old dilapidated building that looked like it had once been a church.

She figured that the person chasing her would know his way around the woods, and she didn't so she decided not to take the chance, and enter the building instead.

The beams had collapsed so she had to crawl through what had once been a doorway; scanning her surroundings, she saw broken stairs leading to nothing.

Getting to her knees, she crawled into a small opening where the roof had caved, along with some more beams; she crawled over to the dark corner where she would be concealed.

She managed to stand in the corner, back against the one wall; eyes on the opening she had crawled through.

She held her breath as she heard footsteps.

Her blood ran cold as her phone vibrated in her pocket; with shaking hands she switched it off and shoved it back into her pocket, hoping the hooded figure had not heard it.

She frowned, she couldn't hear him anymore; maybe he was gone.

Taking a step forward, her forehead hit against something cold and clamming.

She took her phone out and held it up, using the light as a torch.

Hanging from above her head was a hand, the rest of the body concealed.

Screaming she spun, right into the hooded figure.

Swinging her fist, he caught it, pulling her closer, "London, calm down, it's okay."

She froze, "Moth."

He let go of her hands and took the phone from her hands.

Leaning around her, he used her phone to see what she had seen; he inhaled sharply, "C'mon. Whoever did that could still be around."

He took hold of her hand and led her out a way she hadn't even seen.

Keeping hold of her hand they jogged back to the burnt house.

It was only once she stopped moving that she registered the aching from her ankle.

Moth started pacing, "What the hell were you doing, London?"

Kane sighed, "I heard a scream, so I followed it. I didn't realize it was you following me when I got caught in that fence, so I panicked."

Moth stopped, "You got caught in the fence, right. Sit."

Kane rolled her eyes, "I'm fine."

"Sit."

Kane took a step back, suddenly not so sure about Moth, and knocked her leg against the chair in the room, "Ow."

Moth smirked, "Fine hey? Sit down."

Sighing, she sat, "There's a body out there, I think my leg

can wait."

Moth crouched and rolled up her jeans, "She's dead; we can't help her. You are very much alive."

Kane sighed; Moth was extremely close to her, and she started fidgeting.

"Can you stop moving? It's pretty deep; I think you might need stitches."

"No. Hospitals and I don't go."

Moth stood, "Well they do now. Get up, we're going."

"But the-"

"Dead girl, yes I know; we'll call the cops once we get to the hospital."

"But-"

"Nothing. Come." He grabbed her by the wrist and pulled her to her feet, keeping a firm grip on her as they walked out as if he thought she was going to run.

Kane limped behind, "And we're going to walk there? Makes sense."

"No, we're not."

"Was that sarcasm?"

He stopped in front of a black Harley with flames on the tank.

Kane's mouth dropped open, "A Harley? How the hell can you afford that when you live in a-"

He turned abruptly; causing Kane to freeze in mid-sentence.

"Could you stop insulting me?"

Kane bit her bottom lip, "Sorry."

He placed a helmet on her head and she got on behind him, holding onto the back of the bike.

"London, you can hold onto me; I don't bite."

Kane sighed but placed her hands around his waist.

And a few minutes later they were at the hospital; Moth

dragging Kane in by the wrist.

Kane frowned, "I'm not going to run away, you know."

"Good to know; I'm getting used to having you around."

Kane was quite surprised to hear that coming from him, but before she could say anything, they were at the desk.

The woman looked up, "How can I help?"

"She needs stitches."

She handed them a form, "Fill that in first, and wait for-"

Moth cut the woman off, "No. We'll see a doctor now. Her leg is bleeding badly."

He scanned the room and dragged her towards a doctor.

"She needs stitches," he turned to Kane, "I'll call the cops."

The doctor looked between them.

"I'll be right in."

The doctor nodded and walked into one of the rooms.

"Kane, I'm not telling them you found the body. I won't even tell them we were together; you just hide that wound of yours."

"No. Are you crazy? If they think you were alone, they'll blame you."

"I don't want you involved."

"I am involved, whether you like it or not."

Moth sighed, "London, please."

"No. We tell them the truth."

"Fine. Whatever. Go get your leg sorted."

Kane nodded and went in after the doctor.

He introduced himself as Doctor Meyers before injecting her ankle and starting on the stitches.

Kane frowned, looking around the dimly lit room; she was still rather shaken from the night's events.

The doctor looked up, and she screamed, diving backwards; hitting her shoulder on the metal tray, and her head on the wall.

The door flew open and Moth rushed in, crouching beside her, "What happened?"

"Nothing, I, uh..."

Moth turned to the doctor, "Give us a minute."

Without a word, the doctor walked out.

Moth turned back to her, "What happened, London?"

"He, when he looked up, it wasn't his face I saw; it was a burnt and oozing skeleton."

Moth frowned, "Are you okay?"

"Yeah, I'm fine."

Moth took her and they got to their feet, walking out together.

And they came face to face with sheriff Hartley.

"I need your statement, Kane."

"Shouldn't that be Miss London to you?"

He glared at them, "You two had time to get your stories straight?"

Kane smiled, "About as much time as you and a certain Miss Matthews have had to come clean."

His face fell.

Moth frowned at her, unsure of what was going on.

Rick cleared his throat, "I don't know what you mean, Miss London. How about we get that statement done?"

"Sure."

Moth placed his hand on the bottom of her back briefly, "I'll wait at the desk."

Once he walked away, she sat; Rick sitting across from her.

"Look, Kane, you don't want to involve yourself with some-one like Moth, just be honest with me."

"I think it's a bit hypocritical that you're lecturing me about honesty when you're cheating with your nephew's hussy."

"Shut your mouth, you don't know anything."

She smiled, "Sure. Now let's get this over with."

She gave her statement and went over to where Moth waited at the desk, "All done."

"You feeling okay?"

She shrugged.

Moth dropped her off at home.

She walked in and Alice was waiting.

"Where have you been? Do you see the time? Was that the Star boy again?" she frowned, taking in Kane's appearance, "What happened? He did this, didn't he?"

Kane sighed, "Hospital. Yes, I can tell the time. Yes, it was Moth. I chased something and ended up finding a dead body. Yes, I am okay. No, he didn't do this to me; he took me to the hospital."

"A dead body? Where?"

"An old church on Misty Hill."

Alice let out a shaky breath, "You are not to be out after dark. No more going near Misty Hill. And stay away from Moth.'

"Not going to happen, Alice."

"Stay away from him before you end up dead too!"

"Moth is not a killer. And you have no right accusing him." She stormed into her room, slamming the door behind her.

Leaning against it, she let out a shaky breath; the truth of the matter was that she had no idea if he was innocent.

Everything kept replaying in her head; finding the body in the church, the doctor's face changing.

"What's happening to me?"

"You know what.'

She jumped at the voice, "No. I'm not going back there; you're not real."

She was relieved when she was met with silence.

She got her clothes and went to shower' hoping a nice hot shower would clear her mind.

The water turned to blood for a few seconds.

Getting up, she went through to the kitchen and made a cup of coffee. She heard a plop, and when she looked down, it was moving.

She dipped her finger in, it came out red and sticky.

she pushed the cup away and stood. This would be a long night.

3

Chapter 3

Alice came through in the morning.

Kane was still at the counter.

"You're up early."

"I couldn't sleep."

Alice sat down, "Please stay away from Moth."

Kane sighed, "Can you just leave Moth alone?"

"You need to stay away from him."

"I can look after myself, Alice."

Kane got up and went to shower, changing into black bootleg jeans, high heeled ankle boots and a black shirt with a flaming skull on it.

She decided to put on black eye makeup and add red lipstick before adding skull earrings on her way out the door.

When she walked into class, a total of five minutes late, Veda glared at her.

She sat down before greeting Brent.

Once again, the day went by alright until lunch.

She sat at her usual table with her friends.

"What happened?"

"Moth attacked you?"

"You saw him kill a girl?"

This was all of them in unison.

Kane frowned, "No, to all of those. I chased someone and found a body. Moth showed up and took me to the hospital. Where did you hear all that other rubbish?"

"Veda." Replied Macy.

Kane was on her feet and in front of Veda in a second.

Veda raised an eyebrow, still sporting a heavy bruise, "Look what trash the cat dragged in."

Kane narrowed her eyes, "I clearly didn't hit you hard enough, you cheap skank."

Veda smiled, "If you touch me again, I will lay charges."

Kane shrugged, "Oh, I don't want to come too close, especially after you've been doing God knows what with Sheriff Hartley."

The whole table, and the ones close enough to hear, went silent.

Veda went white.

Brent frowned, "What?"

"Your girlfriend has been cheating on you with your uncle."

Veda shook her head, "Brent, she's lying."

Kane took her phone out and handed it to Brent, "Check the videos."

He looked between Kane and Veda before hitting play.

Handing Kane her phone, he stormed out.

Veda glared at Kane, "You're such a bitch."

Kane nodded, "Pretty much."

Layla stood, "Just leave."

Veda also stood, "Yeah, go."

Jack nodded, "Yeah. Before I end up having to hit a girl."

Kane laughed, "You lot do remember how that went the last time, right?"

She felt a tap on her shoulder and turned to see Cliff.

"You don't need to get into any more trouble."

Veda smirked, "Aw, she has brace face looking out for her."

"His name is Cliff."

Veda shrugged, "I don't care."

Kane sighed, "Stacey, you eating this?"

Stacey shook her head with wide eyes.

Kane picked up the tray and threw it at Veda, connecting with her face.

Veda screamed before diving over the table, tackling Kane to the floor, her hands around Kane's throat.

Kane flipped them over and started punching Veda as she desperately tried to get Kane off of her.

Kane caught something out of the corner of her eye, did Cliff just punch Jack?

Was that Macy tackling Layla?

"What in the hell is going on here?"

Everyone froze at the sound of Lewis' voice.

Kane stood, straightening her shirt, "Nothing." She reached over, punching Jack in the face.

"Miss London! All six of you in my office."

They all followed slowly.

Kane shook her head, trying to figure out how she was going to get Cliff and Macy out of this.

When they got to the office, Layla and Veda took the two chairs in front of the desk and Jack took the couch in the corner.

Lewis looked up, "Miss Brown, Mr. Olsen, take a seat."

Kane put a hand over her heart, "You forgot about me."

Lewis narrowed his eyes at her, "Hardly."

Cliff and Macy took a seat next to Jack, Macy between them.

Lewis looked around the room, "Who started this?"

Kane crossed her arms over her chest, "She tackled me."

"You threw a tray at her!"

"Layla, shut up." Hissed Veda.

Lewis turned to Veda, "Did you tackle her?"

"Yes."

"Okay. Detention for a month. And the whole lot of you will be fixing up Misty Hill Asylum."

Kane watched as everyone else in the room went white.

Veda frowned, "But-"

Lewis cut her off, "No buts. All of you will do this. I'll get back to you on dates."

They walked out.

Kane frowned, "What's so bad about the asylum?"

Macy shuddered, "Haunted."

Cliff sighed, "It closed down years ago. No one goes near it because they believe it's haunted. Some people went there and never came back. The patients all died, everyone believes they haunt the place."

Kane frowned, "So why in the hell would we want to fix it up?"

Cliff shrugged, "Maybe they want to re-open it."

Kane didn't say anything; a mental asylum was not something she ever wanted to be near again.

Macy frowned, "Are you okay?"

Kane forced a smile and nodded, "Yeah, just feeling a bit sick. I'm going to ditch and go get some sleep."

She walked away before either of her friends could say anything.

Kane was walking down the road when the voice came back.

"It's ironic."

Kane frowned, "What is?"

"That you'll be fixing up an asylum. Maybe you can pick your own room."

"I'm not crazy."

"Of course you are."

"No."

"Then why are you speaking to me again?"

"Go away!" she shouted, spinning; no one was there.

She sighed and went to the unfinished building; her spot on the roof.

Lying near the stairs, she closed her eyes.

She was woken by terrible screams.

It was only once she had woken up properly that she realized she had been the one screaming; she had been dreaming about her parents.

"Get a grip." She said, getting to her feet and going to the edge of the roof.

It was dark, so she had slept the whole day on the roof.

"You're going crazy."

Kane closed her eyes, "Go away."

"You know you're going crazy again."

"I am not!"

"Is that why you're arguing with something that isn't there?"

Kane let out a shaky breath, "Get a grip, Kane."

"Or take a step."

Kane opened her eyes, looking down she realized she was right on the edge.

"Kane?!"

Kane spun at the sound of Moth's voice, letting out a shrill scream as she fell backwards, off the roof.

Moth dived, grabbed on to one of her wrists just in time.

Kane looked down, "Don't drop me!"

"Stop struggling, London. Give me your other hand."

She reached up and he took hold of her, pulling her back up onto the building.

She clung to him.

"London, what the hell were you thinking?"

She pulled back, "I wasn't planning on falling."

"Please, stay away from the edge of this building."

Kane sighed, "Well, after this, I don't need to be told again."

"What were you doing here anyway?"

"I got into another fight at school. Lewis wants all of us to fix up Misty Hill Asylum, and as you know, that's a bit close to home for me."

Moth had an unreadable look on his face, "Misty Hill Asylum? He must be mad. You're not going near that place."

Kane frowned, "Well it's not like I have a choice. I'm sure I'll be fine, I just need to sort out my mental issues."

"No. People, who go in there, don't come out. That place isn't haunted, it's cursed," he looked up, "And you're not mental."

"I beg to differ."

He frowned, "You're not."

"Tell him how crazy you are."

Kane closed her eyes.

Moth put a hand on her shoulder, "Kane?"

Kane sighed, opening her eyes, "Okay, remember I told you I was in a mental institute? Well, I've started hearing and seeing stuff again. It started when I came to Misty Meadows."

"You aren't crazy," he stood, "Let's get you home."

She sighed, taking his hand as he helped her to her feet and following him down the stairs.

When they reached Alice's gate, Moth paused, wrapping his arms around her, "You're not crazy, I promise you. And please stop walking around at night."

She smiled and went in, not surprised to find Alice glaring at her."

Kane walked past her into the kitchen.

Alice followed, "How many times must I tell you not to hang around that boy?"

Kane rolled her eyes as she opened the fridge, "As many times as you want. I'm still not going to listen though."

"Do you know he's the only suspect in that murder and those disappearances?" Alice followed her closely as she put her plate in the microwave.

"Give me proof that he's guilty and I'll believe you."

"You need to stay away from him? His family brought the curse to Misty Meadows. He's evil."

Kane spun, "There is no curse. His father killed someone, that doesn't make him evil."

Alice grabbed her shoulders, "He brings death with him wherever he goes. He can't be trusted. You must stay away from him."

Kane frowned, "Let go of me."

Alice dropped her hands, "You are in my house, and you abide by my rules."

"Not with this."

"Obviously, my daughter didn't raise you with any discipline, not that I'm surprised–"

Kane cut her off, "I told you not to speak about my mother, you didn't even know her, you didn't even bother coming to the funeral."

Alice's eyes flashed with anger, "If it had only been for her

I would have been there, but I will never set foot in the same place as your father; dead or alive. He was never good enough for her. He was a horrible person, with an attitude to match and you take after him. He should have been the only one to die in that crash, not your mother. No one would have cared; he wasn't worth it."

Kane clenched her teeth, "You bitch."

Alice lifted her hand and slapped Kane across the face.

Kane went closer to Alice, "Don't you ever do that again, next time, I will do it back."

She turned and walked out, going into her room.

The next morning Kane left for school without speaking to Alice; after the night before, she would have liked never to see her again.

As she got to the end of the road, she saw Moth sitting on his bike, waiting on the corner.

Frowning, she went over to him, "What are you doing?"

He smiled, "I was passing by when I thought you might like a lift to school," he frowned, "What happened to your lip?"

Kane rolled her eyes, "Alice slapped me."

Moth narrowed his eyes and clenched his jaw, "Who does she think she is?"

Kane shrugged, "Who cares?"

Moth sighed and shook his head, handing her a helmet.

She put it on and got onto the back.

When she got to class everyone somehow knew Moth had dropped her off.

Cliff lent over his desk, "Did Moth drop you off?"

She nodded.

Veda glared at Kane but said nothing.

The day went by fast and at lunch, Brent joined them at their table.

Brent narrowed his eyes, "Did Moth do that?"

"No, Brent."

Collin sighed, "Oh boy, Mr. Lewis is heading this way."

"Kane, you're needed at the hospital; your grandmother was in an accident."

Kane jumped to her feet, "What?!"

She left, wondering what had happened.

When she finally got to the hospital they allowed her to go straight to Alice.

"What happened, Alice?"

"My brakes stopped working and I went into a truck."

The door opened and Rick walked in.

Rick nodded at Alice and glared at Kane, "We've done some work on your car, and we know the cause. There's no easy way to say this, but it was no accident. Your brake lines were cut."

Kane frowned, "But everyone in this town loves her."

"Not everyone." He said, giving her a pointed look.

Alice sighed, "I can't believe someone wanted to kill me."

Kane turned to Rick, "Any suspects?"

"Two."

"Who?" Asked Alice and Kane in unison.

He looked at Kane, "You and Moth."

Kane frowned, "Me? Have you lost your mind? And Moth has no motive for this."

Rick turned to Alice, "Any enemies?"

Alice glanced at Kane, "No one that I know of."

"I'll be in touch." He gave Kane one last look before walking out.

Kane left soon after, going home.

She made a cup of coffee before going into the back yard.

She stood facing the mass of trees that surrounded the back of the house, thinking of the man she had seen watching her.

She couldn't help but wonder if it had perhaps been Moth.

Her phone rang and she answered, "Hey, Gina."

"Kay! How are you?"

Kane frowned, "What's up, Gina?"

"Um, you remember Goran?"

Kane's hand tightened around the coffee cup; Goran Owens was a name she had hoped never to hear again.

"Yes, Gina. I do."

Gina sighed, "You know I wouldn't mention him unless I had to."

"Get to the point, Gina."

"He's back in town, and he's been asking about you; got into a fight with Scott when he said he doesn't know where you are. He hasn't stopped harassing us; he's hell-bent on finding you."

Suddenly Kane didn't feel so safe standing outside; turning she bolted into the house, closing and locking the door.

Kane hung up and punched the wall.

There was a knock at the door, causing her to jump.

She let out a sigh of relief when she saw it was Moth.

She opened the door and let him in.

"You okay?"

"Fine."

He frowned, "You don't look it."

Kane sighed, going through to the kitchen, "You're a suspect in Alice's attempted murder."

Moth frowned, "Wait, her what? Someone tried to kill her?"

Kane nodded, "Someone messed with her brakes."

"Is she okay?" he asked, taking a seat at the counter.

Kane nodded, "Yeah."

"I can't believe I'm a suspect."

"One of them."

Moth frowned, "Who's the other?"

"Me."

"What? Do you see it? This is why I didn't want you around me," he got to his feet and started pacing.

"I'm innocent, he won't be able to make anything stick," she said, sitting on the counter.

"What part do you not understand? He will target you now for being on my side," he lent on the counter next to Kane, "This is exactly why I didn't want you near me."

Kane scoffed, "A bit late for that now, don't you think?"

Moth looked up and Kane's breath caught as their eyes met.

There was a knock on the door and Moth jumped, "Let me get that for you."

Kane frowned as he walked out, that had been a moment.

Moth returned with Cliff, Collin and Macy in tow.

"How's your gran?"

"She's okay." She replied, trying not to look at Moth.

Collin looked between the two before clearing his throat, "So, are you two going to the fair tonight?"

"Tonight?"

"Yeah, in town–"

There was another knock at the door, this time Macy got it; returning with Brent.

He scanned the room, "Hey."

Macy grinned, "You have awesome timing, we were just talking about the fair."

"Oh? That's actually why I'm here," he turned to Kane, "I wanted to know if you'd like to go with me?"

Macy's smile broadened, "Oh, she'd love–"

Cliff cut her off, "We're all going together, so you're welcome to join us."

Kane smiled, Cliff was becoming quite the lifesaver.

Brent nodded, "Uh, yeah, sure."

Kane turned to Moth, "You're going, right?"

Moth looked amused, "I normally stay away from the people in this town, did you forget?"

Brent scoffed, "Well it's not like any of the people want you there."

Moth ignored him, keeping his eyes on Kane, "I'm going to get going. Stay away from the sheriff." He walked out without another word.

"So what time are we going?" Asked Brent.

"Seven." Replied Macy.

"Great, see you there." He said before walking out.

Macy clapped, "Kane, I get to pick your outfit."

Kane shook her head, "I'm not feeling into it anymore."

Cliff sighed, "Don't worry, Moth will be there."

Kane frowned, "How do you know?"

"He can't seem to stay away from you."

Kane stood glaring at Macy, "There is no way in hell you're picking my outfit; you'll make me look like a ballerina."

Macy huffed and Kane laughed; she looked ridiculous in a white and red summer dress to her knees, cowboy boots and pig-tails.

Kane shook her head, "You look ridiculous."

"It's the theme, Kane."

Kane sighed, "Okay, but I'm not going to look anything like that. I do have an idea though, so go wait for me in the lounge."

Macy rolled her eyes and walked out.

Kane left her hair down in waves and applied a smoky eye

with clear gloss.

She decided on a black body-con dress and added in black and silver cowboy boots

She went out with her hands on her hips, "Approved?"

Macy smiled, "Wow, you look great."

They decided to walk into town where the fair was being held.

Brent nudged her, "You look nice."

"Thanks." She knew it was a conversation killer, but he wasn't the one she wanted to hear that from.

Macy pulled her aside when they got to the fair, "Kane, try to have fun and forget about Moth."

Kane said nothing as Collin whisked Macy away to dance.

Kane went over to Cliff who was staring at Cassie, "Cliff, go ask her to dance."

"Are you crazy?"

Kane grabbed him by the arm and dragged him over to Cassie, "Hey, Cassie, Cliff would like a dance."

Cassie smiled, "I'd love to."

Kane smiled and left them to it.

She lent against one of the stall counters, surprised to see Rick and Veda dancing together.

Suddenly Brent was next to her, "I need a dance partner."

She hesitated before accepting his hand and following him to the make-shift dance floor.

They were a few seconds into the dance when Cassie and Cliff came up next to them.

Cliff nudged her, "Told you he couldn't stay away," he tilted his head and Kane followed with her eyes; there stood Moth in black jeans and a long-sleeved black shirt.

Brent shook his head, "Will he ever figure out where he isn't wanted."

Kane smiled, "I'm just glad he figured out where he is wanted." She let go of Brent and went over to Moth.

She smiled at him, "Hey, you came."

He smiled and started to speak but she wasn't listening to him; she was listening to the voice whispering in her ear.

"House of Horrors, blood will run."

She turned to the House of Horrors set up and frowned, there was a girl with long black hair staring straight at her.

Suddenly the girl's head snapped back, revealing a deep cut on her neck.

And then she was gone.

Without a word, Kane started running toward the House of Horrors.

Moth frowned but ran after her.

"London?"

Keep going

Kane continued with Moth close behind.

Hurry, before it's too late

Kane carried on, ignoring the props placed to scare people.

Stop

She stopped, looking up at the dolls hanging from the ceiling.

"Oh, God."

Moth grabbed her arm, "What is it?"

Suddenly blood dripped down onto Moth and he looked up to see the girl with black hair, her neck slit open.

Moth sighed, "And we had to be the ones to find her."

Kane shook her head and they went to find Rick.

After they had told him everything, Moth went home with Kane.

He sat across from her at the counter, after she had told him how she had known to look for the girl.

He stood and motioned for her to follow him, stopping at the couch, "Get some sleep, you look tired."

"I won't be able to sleep with all this going on."

Moth sat on the one chair in the corner, "Sleep. I'll stay here till you wake up."

4

Chapter 4

Kane awoke to noises in the kitchen.

Getting to her feet she went into the kitchen to find Alice making breakfast.

"Where's-"

"He went home, he was tired. Found him sitting in the lounge staring at you when I got home. He told me what happened at the fair."

Kane sat down at the counter, "And?"

Alice turned, "And what?"

Kane raised a brow, "No lecture?"

"It's your life to mess up." She turned back to the eggs in the pan.

Kane dressed and left for school.

She was walking down the road when a woman with a hole in her heart appeared in front of her; the woman had long brown hair and a white nightgown on, dark circles around her eyes.

Kane froze, "What the hell?"

"You need to stay away from him," she said.

"Who?"

"It's a curse."
Kane frowned, "What is?"
And just as she had appeared, the woman vanished.
*
The moment she set foot in school, she was called to Mr. Lewis' office.
She went in, closing the door behind her.
"Kane, have a seat please."
Kane frowned but sat.
"I hear Alice is out of the hospital."
Kane nodded.
"She mentioned to me that a friend of yours is coming to visit for the holiday, I've agreed to let her join you for the Asylum project."
Kane frowned, "We're going to be there for a whole two weeks?"
"Yes. You will stay there and help with the renovations, just some painting and fixing things."
Kane didn't like the sound of this at all.
She nodded.
"Great. You start on Monday."
Six days away; she wanted to tell him no and explain, but other than Moth, no one knew about her time in the asylum.
"Great. Monday. Can I get to class now?"
Lewis nodded and she walked out.
Going into the class, she sat down.
Cliff lent over, "Did Lewis tell you?"
Kane nodded.
"Should be interesting."
Kane kept her mouth firmly shut.
Macy sat down, "I'm not looking forward to it."

Kane nodded, "Makes two of us."

Cliff frowned, "It could be fun."

Macy scoffed, "Two weeks in a madhouse? Doubt that would be anything other than hell."

Kane nodded again, "Hell would be more fun."

Cliff frowned at her, "There's something you're not telling us."

Kane shook her head, "No there isn't."

But as the class began, Kane couldn't help thinking back to her six months in that mental institute; it had been the worst six months of her life, locked in a small white room for the first three months, she had been made to wear a straight jacket for the first two.

Everyone looking at her like she was crazy, the doctors had kept her so sedated that she had been in a zombie-like state, prodding her with needles, even going as far as trying shock therapy.

And the patients, they were the worst; some had ganged up and tried to sacrifice her, fully believing that she was a demon sent from hell, to kill them and the rest of the Christians.

It had gotten to a point that she had just pretended to stop hearing and seeing things, just to get out.

But, with three months of pretending, she had stopped hearing and seeing things, and she had begun to believe that maybe she had been crazy and the doctors had healed her.

She had been sitting outside, waiting for her parents to arrive when one of the patients had come up to her.

"Kane, right?"

Kane had nodded.

"I saw him last night, I saw him."

Kane had frowned at the other girl but had not said anything, not knowing what she was meaning.

"The man that talks to you; he came to my room last night and told me to give you a message, he said you will never be rid of him; your family has the curse. He said that you will never be free until you-"

And that's when a nurse had run up, telling her that her parents had been in an accident.

She had gotten to her feet and followed the nurse to the office where she was told that her parents were in the hospital and she would be taken there; she had been so drugged that she had felt nothing.

She had calmly walked into the hospital, and when the doctor had told her that her parents were dead, she felt nothing.

She had wanted to scream, to cry, anything, but she hadn't been able to, it was like watching it happen to someone else.

She had gone in to see the bodies of her parents, but still; she felt nothing.

She had picked up her mother's limp hand and felt no emotion.

She stared at their bruised faces and felt no sadness.

When she left the hospital, she had been taken to Gina's house and sitting on the bed with her pills in front of her, she had decided then to stop taking them; she started to think that she had been fine before, and it was those pills that had made her truly crazy.

Sitting in class, she tried to think back to when she had started seeing and hearing things, but she couldn't seem to pinpoint an exact time; for as long as she could remember, it was always there.

A voice telling her when things would happen; seeing things that would happen.

But those pills had stopped her from seeing the warning of her parents; if she had been of a normal mind, she would have seen it and been able to warn them.

At lunch, Kane sat hoping for some calamity.

Of course, with her friends, that wouldn't happen.

"Spill, K."

Kane glared at Cliff, "Nothing to spill."

Macy's attention was elsewhere, "What is he doing back?"

Kane turned to see Moth heading straight for them.

Cliff laughed, "Like I said, he can't stay away from Kane."

He stopped, frowning down at Kane, "It's a real bitch trying to get into this place when you're no longer a student."

Brent sat, "Especially when it's you."

Moth ignored him, keeping his attention on Kane, "You feeling okay?"

Kane nodded, not sure what else to do considering she most certainly did not feel okay.

Cliff cleared his throat, "We're starting with the asylum in six days."

Moth nodded, he was not impressed, he turned to Kane, "I'll pick you up after school."

They watched as he walked away and Macy pursed her lips, "That guy is trouble."

Kane rolled her eyes, "At least he's sweet."

"As if a guy who was on trial for manslaughter can be anything else." Said, Macy.

Cliff turned to Brent, "So, two weeks with your ex."

Brent glared at him, "Since when did you get a backbone?"

Kane kicked him under the table, "Watch it."

Before Brent could give a reply, Cassie stood beside the table with a shy smile on her face, "Can I sit?"

Kane grinned at Cliff, "Of course."

Macy smiled, looking impressed, "Looks like Veda might be losing followers."

Cassie giggled, "Oh, yes, especially now that Kane's in the running for Best Looking Student of The Year."

Kane frowned, "What?"

Macy's eyes went the size of saucers.

"Macy, what did you do?"

She shrugged, "Well, I may have entered you."

Kane glared at her, "I want to kill you right now."

Cassie nudged her, "Relax; you'll knock Veda off her perch with no hassle."

Kane rolled her eyes and took a bite of her chocolate cupcake.

Cassie lent forward, "So, what's going on with you and Moth?"

Kane shrugged.

Cassie raised her brows, "Looks like you have something going on between you too."

Kane shook her head, "We don't."

Cliff gave her a look, "Yet."

Brent scoffed.

Kane raised a brow, "Oh look, I have my own commentary," she frowned, "How did I end up with such dorks?"

Macy grinned, "You need some light and joy in your life."

"Freaks."

"That's why you love us."

Kane rolled her eyes and lent over to steal half of Macy's sandwich.

Kane walked out of the school doors and immediately saw Moth standing next to his Harley.

He smiled as she came up to him, "How was school?"

"Boring. How was work?"
"Boring. Let's go." He stepped forward with a helmet.
Kane tilted her head, "I could walk home."
"You're not going home just yet."
"Where are we going?"
"It's a surprise, London; now let's go."

5

Chapter 5

Moth had taken her to a cliff.

Kane set the helmet on the bike and scanned the area, "Where are we."

"The only place in Misty Meadows that isn't haunted."

"Well, it's beautiful."

"I scattered my mother's ashes here."

Kane wasn't sure what to say to that, so she looked around, desperate for something that would change the subject and she lamely settled on, "It's really pretty."

Moth nodded, and awkwardly pulled out a gold chain with a gold ankh pendant and held it out to her, "It's supposed to ward off evil and stuff. My mom swore it protected her from the town, she lost it a few days before she died, and I found it today and thought you might like it."

"Wow, thank you."

Moth took the chain and came up behind her, placing the chain around her neck.

He stayed there and rested his hands on her shoulders, "London, don't go into that asylum. People don't come out of there; I can't lose you too."

Kane's blood ran cold, but she turned to face him, "My friends are going in there and I can't leave them to face this alone."

Moth shook his head, "Please just think of you with this."

"No, I can't just leave-"

Moth cut her off, his lips against hers.

Kane jumped back, "What the hell was that?"

"Well, you kissed me back."

Kane frowned, "You just kissed me."

He nodded.

Her phone started ringing and she answered without looking at it, "Hello?"

"Kay, long time."

She froze; that was a voice she had hoped to never hear again.

Goran Owens; her psychotic ex.

"What do you want, Goran?"

"I just called to tell you I miss you, I'm hurt that you left without even saying goodbye."

Kane realized she must have looked as freaked out as she felt because Moth had a concerned look on her face.

"Kane, why so quiet?"

Kane exhaled a shaky breath, "You need to leave me alone; I want nothing to do with you."

What he said next turned Kane's blood to ice.

"You thought running off to Misty Meadows would keep me away? The town is so small, sweetheart; I'll be seeing you soon," he paused, "And tell that flame obsessed freak not to even try standing in my way."

She dropped the phone, looking around in a panic.

"London, what was that about?"

Kane shook her head, "Nothing."

"Right; that's why you've gone as pale as a ghost. Tell me what's going on." He picked up the phone and studied it as if the phone would tell him.

Kane sighed, "Goran Owens; He's an ex of mine, he's crazy I have a restraining order on him, but he still stalks me. He's here and he knows about you and he's not very happy."

"Stalks? New rule; you go nowhere without me, or one of the other three. If you see him anywhere, you tell me. Give me a description so I know who I'm looking out for. And speak to Alice so she knows too."

Kane frowned, "Hold up, this guy is a whole new level of crazy; he won't think twice of killing someone."

"Which is why I won't let him come anywhere near you."

When they got to Alice's, Moth stayed with Kane to make sure she told Alice everything.

Alice agreed with Moth that Kane wasn't to go anywhere alone, and she invited Moth to stay for dinner.

When Kane went to bed, Moth was still there.

He went into the kitchen to talk to Alice, now that Kane was in her room.

"Alice, I know my father wasn't a good person, but I am not like him."

Alice turned to him with a grim look on her face, "Evil follows your family like a plague. You say you are not like your father, yet you seem to follow his footsteps."

"But that isn't true."

Alice raised a brow, "You were both accused of murder."

"The difference is that he was guilty, and I'm not."

Alice shook her head, "In the eyes of the town, you were both guilty."

"I don't care what this town thinks of me, I care about what

Kane thinks of me, and at the moment she believes that I'm innocent and that's all I need. You don't have to believe it, but I care about Kane."

"You cared about Willow too, didn't you? But she still ended up dead in that fire on Misty Hill."

Moth said nothing, keeping his face void of any emotion; even though her words cut deep.

Willow Hillson had died in the house on Misty Hill along with his father, Kal Star and a few others.

Moth hadn't known she was in the house until he had been asked to identify the body.

He couldn't help but think back to that night, standing on that hill, watching as the house burnt down; people screaming around him.

Alice frowned, "You've gone pale; sit down."

Moth took a seat at the counter and shook his head, "Look, if Goran has been watching Kane, and he knows me, he knows you too, so he'll know that she's staying here."

"Yes, I've thought of that."

"Well, I'll be here as much as I can. As long as you'll allow me."

Alice nodded, "That's fine; there's a sleeper couch in the lounge that you're welcome to use. Also, I want you to go with her to that asylum."

Moth nodded, "I was planning on it."

"I'll speak to Lewis and explain why I want you there."

"Tell him I'll be bringing a guy named Kelso; I'm not taking any risks with Owens around."

"I'll go and see him first thing in the morning."

"Kelso will go with you; if Owens is around he might target you too."

Alice shook her head, "I'll be just fine."

"Neither of you will be alone until this guy has stopped."

Alice nodded, "Okay, I'll go check on Kane and then bring you some blankets."

Moth waited till Alice was out of the room before letting out a breath; trying to forget that burning house.

When he closed his eyes, he could still see Willow's charred body.

Kane woke up the next morning and frowned when she saw Moth in the chair in the corner of the room with a coffee mug in his hands.

"You stayed the whole night?"

Moth nodded, "Yeah, and I've gotten my friend Kelso to stick around to make sure Alice is safe."

Kane's frown deepened, "She can't be too happy with you being here."

Moth laughed, "She's fine with it; where do you think I got the coffee from?"

Kane smiled, "Well, lucky she can't make up her mind then."

"She's making breakfast with Kelso; I think we might have had a breakthrough."

Kane was surprised but happy to hear this.

She got up and went to the kitchen with Moth close behind.

Alice stood at the stove making pancakes with a tall guy with messy, longish brown hair, who stood stirring a bowl of batter.

Kane let out a laugh, "That looks hilarious."

He looked up with a smile, "You must be Kane. I'm Kelso."

Kane sat at the counter, pushing her phone away when a private number called.

Moth answered and hit speaker's phone.

"What's up?"

Silence.

Alice and Kelso turned to look at the phone, while Kane and Moth kept their eyes on each other.

Moth tilted his head, "Can I help you?"

"I want to speak to Kane." She could hear the anger in Goran's voice.

"Who can I say is calling?"

"Her boyfriend."

"Her boyfriend, give her the phone."

Moth hung up.

Kane stood, "I'm going to get ready for school."

She got her clothes and went to the bathroom; she filled the tub and climbed in.

Leaning her head back, she closed her eyes; enjoying the warm water.

Plop

Kane tried to ignore the sound.

She frowned; the water had gotten a lot thicker.

Her eyes flew open and she let out a scream, jumping to her feet and trying to get out of the thick blood that now filled the tub.

She slipped and fell, hitting her arm and leg hard against the tiled floor, and her head against the wall.

She instantly felt light-headed.

Looking up, she saw the charred girl she had seen in the mirror in the house on Misty Hill.

Leaning up, Kane pulled the towel and covered herself, and the charred girl reached out a hand to her at the same time the door opened and Moth stood there, "London, are you okay?"

The girl's eye widened in shock at the sight of him... or was that fear.

Kane frowned, "I, uh, fell."

Alice barged in, pushing past Moth.

'Kane, are you okay?"

She pulled herself to her feet, readjusting the towel to keep it in place.

Moth came forward, "You're bleeding!"

Alice shoved him out, "Lounge; I'll take care of this." She closed the door in his face and turned back to Kane, "Now, tell me what happened."

"I fell."

Alice gave her a look, "You screamed."

"Because I fell."

Alice didn't look like she believed that, but she sighed and said, "We need to get you to the hospital."

Kane nodded, "I'll get changed and we can go."

Alice walked out and Kane changed into her clothes, rolling the sleeves of her shirt up so it wasn't rubbing against the cut on her forearm.

She walked out to see Moth leaning against the wall with his arms crossed over his chest.

"You okay?"

Kane sighed, "The water in the bath turned to blood and a burnt girl appeared."

His eyes flashed, "Burnt girl?"

Kane nodded, "It's the second time I've seen her; the first was in the mirror at that house you sleep in."

Moth paled and opened and closed his mouth a few times.

But before Kane could get anything out of him, Kelso came to them to let them know that Alice was waiting to take Kane to the hospital.

Kane sat on a hospital bed with Doctor Meyers standing in

front of her; Alice, Kelso and Moth were in the waiting room.

"Well, the good news is that you don't have a concussion, bad news is that we need to stitch this up. I must say, Miss London, trouble seems to follow you."

Kane nodded, "It sure does."

'Or maybe it follows Moth'

Kane frowned but said nothing; she wasn't about to argue with a voice only she could hear.

"Can I rather just bandage it and keep it clean?"

He nodded, "You can, but it will take longer to heal."

"That's fine," she frowned, thinking of the last time she had seen the Doctor, "Is there a shrink around?"

His movements slowed slightly, "Why?"

"Oh, I'm just asking."

"That isn't something one would ask for the fun of it."

Kane sighed, "Okay, I think I need one."

He frowned, "And why is that?"

"I, uh, see things that others don't."

Meyers tilted his head slightly, "And how do you know that others don't see them? Or that seeing them makes you crazy?"

Kane frowned, "Well, I mean…"

"Don't underestimate the town, Miss London; it doesn't have the reputation of being haunted for no reason."

"You don't even know what I've been seeing."

The Doctor chuckled, "Dead people, perhaps?"

Kane sighed and explained everything, from her time in the mental institute, right up to how she had gotten the cut on her arm.

Meyers smiled, "Both of your grandmothers were born here; both of your grandfathers were born here; both of your parents were born here. There are at least ten generations of Gomes, and three to four generations of London's in this town; have you ever stopped to think that maybe you were brought back here for a reason? Others may think that you need help; I think you have a gift."

Kane said nothing; she hadn't expected that from the doctor at all.

When he was done, she thanked him and walked out.

Moth was the first at her side "Is everything okay?"

Kane nodded.

Alice came over to them, "I've already contacted Lewis and told him you won't be coming in; Kelso is waiting in the car, we need to go see the sheriff about Goran."

Kane rolled her eyes, "That guy hates me; he's not going to be much help."

Alice turned to Moth, "Maybe it would be best if you weren't with us."

"If Moth isn't there, I'm not going."

Alice said nothing as she walked out.

As Kane and Moth followed, he reached out and took hold of her hand.

After they had been to the station and spoken to Rick, Kane was sure he wasn't planning on doing anything about Goran.

Kane sat in the lounge staring at the television but not paying attention; Moth sat watching her.

Alice walked in, "I need to do some shopping, Kelso and I won't be long."

Moth nodded; waiting until Alice and Kelso had left before turning back to Kane.

"You said you saw a burnt girl; what did she look like?"

Kane frowned, "Charred."

Moth exhaled, hoping she wouldn't notice the effect her

words had on him; he had a good idea of who she was seeing, but he couldn't tell her that.

If she knew...

Kane stood, "What aren't you telling me?"

Moth shook his head, avoiding her gaze, "Nothing."

"Moth, I'm not stupid."

He pulled out his lighter, flicking it on and off, "Leave it alone, London."

She crossed her arms over her chest, "In case you missed it, I'm not good at taking orders. You know something about that girl I've been seeing, and I want to know what it is."

He jumped to his feet, clearly angry, "Just leave it!"

"No! You aren't the one getting haunted by her, so-"

"How do you know I'm not being haunted by her?"

Kane frowned, "Why would she haunt you? How are the two of you connected?"

Moth sighed, "She died on the fire on Misty Hill along with my father."

Kane froze as she remembered the girls fear-filled eyes in the bathroom when she had heard Moth's voice.

Why would she be scared of Moth; unless he had been responsible for the fire?

She thought back to the woman with the hole in her chest, telling her to stay away from 'him'; was it Moth?

Moth spoke, his voice pulling her from her thoughts, "Don't do that, London, please, don't look at me like the rest of Misty Meadows; like I'm a monster."

Kane frowned, had she been looking at him like that? Had she made him feel as if she felt the same way everyone else did?

She hoped she hadn't, but she didn't know exactly what she thought anymore.

As much as she didn't want to admit it, there was a part of her screaming for her to believe what everyone had said about him; screaming at her to get away from him.

But, of course, there was also the part of her that trusted him with her life; wanting to believe he was innocent.

Kane sighed, "You know I would never look at you like everyone else."

He didn't miss a beat, "There was a second there that you did."

Before she could reply, there was a knock at the door, and Moth went to get it, while she tried to convince herself that Moth wasn't a monster.

Moth returned with Brent, Cassie, Cliff, Collin and Macy.

"Are you okay?" Of course, Cliff would be the first to ask her.

She nodded, filling them in on Goran Owens, and everything else they had missed.

Macy looked rather worried, "What if he does get to you, Kane?"

Moth spoke before she could, "I won't let that happen."

Brent scoffed, "You can't guarantee that."

Moth glared at him, "I know I can."

Brent narrowed his eyes, "Somehow I doubt that."

Cliff rolled his eyes, "Funny, you've been convinced he's some dangerous killer, now you don't think he'll be able to protect Kane."

"Excuse me, I'm standing right here, and I can protect myself," she turned, noticing how Cassie stood awkwardly away from them, she turned back to Cliff, "Brace-Face, you've got to get your girl to come out of her shell a bit," she turned back to Cassie, "Sorry, you're just a bit too quiet."

Moth instantly picked up she was ready to change the subject and went along with it.

He motioned to himself, "Yeah, you have the accused killer," he motioned to Cassie and Cliff, 'The nerd dating the ex popular girl," moving on to Collin and Macy he said, 'The secret couple, who isn't so secret," he grunted in Brent's direction, 'The self-obsessed, arrogant Jock," lastly he motioned to Kane, "And the big mouth bad girl no one wants to cross," he turned back to Cassie, "With this normal group, how can you even think of being quiet?"

Kane frowned, "Bigmouth bad girl? That's the best you could do?"

Moth seemed to be thinking for a second, "Okay, let's rephrase that, the accused killer and resident bad boy, and then not to be messed with bad girl, who seems to be avoiding speaking of her kiss with the said accused killer."

Kane's mouth dropped and her eyes widened, had he just said that?

All eyes were on her.

Macy looked at Kane, "When did this happen?"

Brent glared at Moth.

Cliff high fived him, "It's about time you woke up and made a move."

Kane could not believe he had just told everyone about their kiss.

And right on cue, Alice and Kelso walked in.

Alice frowned, "Why do you lot all look as if you've seen a ghost?"

Kane winced at her choice of words.

Cliff put on a huge smile, "Oh, nothing, Mrs. Gomes."

Brent had other plans, "Kane and Moth are dating."

Collin sighed, "Oh God." Kane cleared her throat, about to

try and fix the situation, but Alice spoke.

"Yes, thank you, Brent, but I've pretty much figured that out for myself."

Kane and Moth exchanged glances, "What?"

Alice sighed, "I might be old, but I'm not stupid; with the way you two have been lately, it is quite obvious."

Kane frowned, "We aren't dating."

Moth gave her a look, "Yet."

Brent was not amused, "This is ridiculous! He's a killer!"

Alice turned to him, "Excuse me, but this is my house, and I expect a bit more respect than that. It's no secret that I'm not very fond of Moth, but none of us know what happened on that hill and cannot make assumptions on hearsay. Besides, Kane is happy."

There was an extremely awkward pause; no one could believe Alice was standing up for Moth.

Cassie cleared her throat, "There's a get together at the lake tonight. Mrs. Gomes, do you think it would be fine if Kane joined us?"

Moth spun, "The lake; are you crazy?"

Kane frowned, "What's wrong with the lake?"

Collin frowned, "It's also haunted."

Kane thought back to her first day in Misty Meadows when the water in the lake had turned to blood.

"Why is it haunted?"

Macy took the chance to answer, "This one guy ran out of the burning house on Misty Hill, covered in flames and he threw himself in the lake, trying to put out the flames; but it was too late and his body was found in the lake a few days later."

Kane sighed, "This town just gets better and better."

Brent cleared his throat, "It's going to be awesome, and

everyone from school is going."

Kane shrugged, "I guess it could be fun."

Alice frowned, "Is it a good idea with Goran around?"

Brent nodded, "Yeah, we'll-"

Moth spoke as if Brent wasn't even there, "I'll make sure he doesn't come anywhere near her."

Kane had gone for a plain look for their outing at the lake; black boots, dark blue jeans and a long-sleeved button up red and black plaid shirt.

Moth and Kane left Kelso to keep Alice safe; there was no telling where Goran would strike.

When they got to the lake, Kane was surprised to see just how many people were there.

There was also a huge bonfire.

Moth sighed, "Me near flames; they're going to have a field day."

Kane rolled her eyes, "Good for them, at least they'll have something to talk about."

Macy came over in heels too high and a white dress.

"I'm so glad you came!"

"You're the only one," said Kane as she eyed the preppy group around her.

Moth looked around, "Where's Cassie and Cliff?"

"They went with Collin to get something to drink. Kane, have you seen Brent yet?"

Kane shook her head, "No, why?"

"He looks so good! Talk about eye candy!"

Kane scrunched her nose up in disgust, "Ew, no thanks; he's the male version of a Barbie doll."

Moth cleared his throat, "And here he comes."

Kane turned to see Brent; he was in blue jeans, a white polo shirt with white sneakers, his sun-kissed hair slicked back neatly.

Kane shook her head; she and Moth were the only two who didn't look preppy.

Brent smiled at her, "The Best Looking Student is tomorrow, you might want to network for some votes."

Kane laughed, "I'll pass, I didn't even want to enter."

Cassie, Cliff and Collin joined them.

Kane smiled, "Nice to see you've toned down the geekiness, Cliff."

Brent laughed, "well he's dating Cass now, he has to step it up."

Cassie sighed, "Brent, don't start."

Kane shot him a look, "He's missing the feeling of my fist in his face."

Moth rested his hand on her lower back, "London, no fights tonight."

Kane sighed, he had a point though.

Macy, who couldn't seem to walk in her heels, dragged Collin off to dance.

Kane caught a glimpse of a tall blond figure and wondered if it was Goran.

Moth frowned, "What's wrong?"

She shook her head, "Nothing."

"You sure?"

She nodded; she wasn't about to ruin the night worrying about Goran.

A few hours into the night and Kane had managed to sneak out of Moth's constant watch.

She was crouched in front of the lake; running her hands through the water when she heard the gravel crunch behind her.

She turned to see a girl with long blond hair, a few years younger than her.

Kane realized she was a ghost when she took in what the girl was wearing; blood-soaked jeans with a once-white shirt.

Kane stood, "Let me guess, your body is here somewhere."

Suddenly screams were coming from the sheds.

Kane ran, pushing her way through the people.

And the sight before her turned her blood to ice; it was the girl she had just seen; she lay on the ground in a pool of blood, her neck sliced open.

Macy was huddled in the corner crying.

Kane crouched next to her, "Mace, are you okay?"

Macy wrapped her arms around Kane and continued to cry.

Soon Rick was called, and Macy gave her statement before leaving with Collin.

Kane had convinced Cliff to take Cassie home, telling him she would be fine.

Moth was by her side when Rick had insisted on questioning her; after which they had gone home and told Alice and Kelso of the night's events.

As Alice spoke with Kelso and Moth about Misty Meadows, Kane sat in silence, trying to find the answer to only one question she had.

Where had Moth been at the time of the murder?

That was something she needed to know; it had been bugging her since finding the girl's body.

Alice stood, "I'm going to get some sleep."

She walked out leaving the three sitting in silence.

Kelso cleared his throat, "So, where were the two of you when she was found?"

"I was at the lake." She turned to Moth.

He looked between the two of them, "I, uh, went to the toilet."

Kane didn't miss the look in Kelso's eyes, and she was sure that Moth didn't miss the look in hers.

She stood, "Goodnight, I need to get some sleep."

Of course, she didn't go to her room; she simply stepped out of sight and listened in on the conversation.

Kelso started speaking, and not in English.

"Cad a rinne to?"

Moth sighed, "Nothing, Kelso."

Kelso rattled off in Celtic.

Little did he know, Kane knew the language; why was he so concerned for her not to hear their conversation?

Moth laughed and changed to Italian, "Lei said irlandese, impara a scuola."

Kane rolled her eyes; he had just told Kelso she learned the language at school.

What Moth didn't know, however, was that she was fluent in Italian, French and Spanish too.

Kelso sounded annoyed and he rattled off in Italian.

Kane frowned, yeah Moth, what did you do?

"Nothing, Kelso."

"Non ti credo."

Kane frowned; getting worried because his friend didn't believe him."

Shaking her head, she decided to go to her room and sleep.

6

Chapter 6

The next morning Kane was up and ready for school.

Moth dropped her at the school gates, and as she got off the bike, she turned to him.

"By the way, those walls that have ears? They know Italian too," She walked into the building, leaving Moth sitting in shock.

She found Cliff sitting under a tree in the back, writing in one of his books.

He looked up as she sat down in front of him.

"Hey, K."

"Hey, where's Cass?"

He sighed, "With Brent and them."

"Ah, so she's not letting go of them just yet?"

"I guess not. But it's okay; we're still good. How are you and Moth?"

"There is no me and Moth, Cliff."

The last thing she wanted was to think of Moth; especially after what had happened the night before.

"Anyone can see the chemistry between you two."

Kane sighed, "I know, but there's a lot of other stuff to consider."

"Like?"

Kane frowned, "I don't even know if I believe in his innocence anymore. I mean, I wasn't there when that fire on Misty Hill happened. And these last murders? Moth could have easily gone off to kill them."

She felt terrible as soon as the words left her mouth, but she needed to tell someone and she knew Cliff was the one she could trust.

Cliff had a deep frown on his face, "Well, what was it that made you believe in his innocence in the first place, Kane?"

"My feelings, I guess."

Cliff nodded, "And you still want to believe he's innocent?"

"Of course."

"Then speak to him and put your mind at ease."

Kane sighed; Cliff thought it was a lot easier than it was.

But she knew very well that it wasn't that simple.

She stood, "I'm going to the library, see you in class."

She knew that no one would be in the library at this time, so it would be the perfect place for her to do some thinking.

Finding a spot near one of the windows, she grabbed a book to make it look as though she was studying in case someone saw her.

As soon as she had sat down, her phone rang.

She answered even though it was a hidden number.

"Hello."

She knew it was Goran even before he spoke.

"You look gorgeous in that black dress."

"Goran, get yourself a life and stop stalking me. Or, grow a pair and come and face me instead of hiding behind a phone."

He gave a low chuckle, "Oh, but watching you is so fun. Especially the way you're sitting in that chair, staring out the window with that cute look on your face, not even reading the book in your lap."

Kane froze, fighting the urge to look around; she now knew he was close, but she refused to let him know he had gotten under her skin.

She scoffed, "Well done, you see me. Would you like a badge?"

"Only if it's signed in your blood; though I'm sure that can be arranged."

Kane had had enough, "You know what? Screw you, you sick and twisted bastard. Instead of making threats while hiding behind a phone, why don't you come out and carry them out? I dare you."

She got to her feet, waiting for any sign of him.

The line had been quiet and when he spoke, she knew she had pushed him too far.

"Kane, do not push me; I am not hiding, I am simply waiting for the right time. Don't forget I plan on showing your freak show boyfriend what I'm capable of first. Should I start with him, or Kelso? But don't worry, when I get my hands on Moth, I'll make sure you're there to watch him die."

Kane hung up, and calmly placed the phone in her bag, walking out slowly; she would not run.

Walking down the hall to her first class, she felt like prey; knowing he was watching her.

She wished he would just show himself; that way she had a chance to fight.

But this game of hiding and seek was getting on her nerves, not to mention she was actually worried about the safety of Alice and her friends.

She walked into class and sat next to Cliff.

"Goran was watching me in the library."

He frowned, "Have you told Moth?"

The teacher walked in before she could reply, and she was happy with that; she didn't want to be thinking of Moth or Goran right now.

The way Kelso had been last night; he had thought that Moth had something to do with the latest murders.

And if his own friend didn't trust him, how could she?

After school, everyone stood in the hall waiting for the announcement on who had won Best Looking Student.

Brent had already been announced as the winner for the males.

The three finalists were Kane, Layla and Veda,

The three of them stood on a makeshift stage; Kane just wanted to leave.

"Third place goes to Layla King."

Kane frowned; she knew Layla was normally second, with Veda in first.

Veda gave Kane a short annoyed glance as Layla took her flowers and stepped off the stage.

"And the winner of this year's Best Looking Female student goes too," Veda stepped forward before the headmaster even finished, "Kane London."

Kane frowned, "what now?'

Veda spun, "No, you must be mistaken."

Mr. Lewis shook his head, "No, she got more votes than you."

Veda glared at Kane, "I've been the winner for three years, you can't just come in here and take over; you're not even better looking than me."

Kane laughed, "Apparently the rest of the school disagrees."

She started for the stairs.

Mr. Lewis frowned, "Kane, your prize?"

Kane turned, "I don't need a piece of plastic and a ribbon to know I'm better than her."

She went over to Collin, Cliff and Macy, and they walked out.

Cliff had a shift at the store they all went with him.

Sitting on the counter, Kane turned to Cliff, "So, how's it going with Cass?"

"Good I guess."

Macy frowned, "You guess?"

"Well, she still hangs out with Veda."

Collin shook his head, "Once a Veda follower, always a Veda follower."

"Who's a Veda follower?" Asked none other than Cassie, as she walked in.

Kane smiled, "You."

Cassie frowned, "I-"

Kane cut her off, "In case you haven't noticed, Cliff here doesn't fit into your little crowd of so-called perfection. You need to either start acting like a proper girlfriend, or get yourself another boyfriend because quite frankly he can do a lot better, and if you plan on treating him like he's your little pet, we're going to have a problem, and I'm sure you're clever enough to know that pissing me off isn't the greatest of ideas. So hurry up and decide what it is you want, but stop toying with him."

Cliff went red.

Cassie was obviously at a loss for words, and she was saved by Rick.

Kane rolled her eyes the moment he walked in.

"Afternoon, Kane, can I have a word?"

"What have I done this time?"

"It's about Goran Owens."

Kane got off the counter and walked out without a word.

Rick followed her and motioned to the other side of the parking lot where they walked to his car, and Kane lent back against the bonnet.

"She crossed her arms, "So, what about Goran?"

"I put the word out, and he's been seen."

Kane sighed, "I know, he called me when I was in the library at school; he was watching me."

"Well, according to the law, I can't arrest him, but I do plan on finding him and giving him a good talk. Oh, and he's related to Mr. Lewis."

"That explains how he got access to the library."

"Yes, well, I'm going to have a chat with Lewis now."

"Okay."

"Well, that's all for now."

Kane started for the store, "Thanks, Rick."

"Oh, and Kane?" he waited for her to turn back to him before continuing, "Watch your back, from Owens and Star."

Before, she would have attacked him for telling her to watch her back from Moth, but now she simply nodded before going back into the store.

Macy raised a brow, "And?"

Kane shrugged, "He was just letting me know that they've seen Goran around and they are still looking for him."

"Well, at least he's helping you."

Kane nodded, she knew it was his job, but she was still surprised that he was actually making an effort.

What surprised her a bit more was that he had sounded genuinely worried about her when he had told her to watch her back.

Kane and Kelso were in the kitchen making supper; Moth had taken Alice for her check-up.

"Kelso, why do you think Moth had something to do with the most recent murders?"

Kelso frowned, "How do you-"

"I know Italian."

Kelso sighed, "Look, Moth has always had a shady past, especially with the law. But he swears he had nothing to do with it, and he wouldn't lie to me."

Kane sighed and turned back to the pot, stirring the chicken.

"He cares about you, Kane."

Kane nodded, "I know."

'It's the curse'

Kane stopped stirring, listening to the female voice.

'More will die'

Kane turned slightly.

'You must stay away or you will be among the dead'

Kane frowned, "Kelso, finish up with dinner; I'm just going to the toilet."

She didn't wait for a reply, going into the bathroom she closed the door and turned.

"Okay, where are you?"

She felt a breath on the back of her neck and dived forward, spinning to see the charred girl.

She knew the voice had not belonged to this girl.

The girl lifted a finger, pointing to Kane's neck.

Kane frowned, "Look, I don't-"

"Kane? Where are you?" Moth was back.

The girl's head whipped towards the sound of his voice, and then suddenly back to Kane.

Her dead eyes literally flashed before she dived forward,

wrapping her hands around Kane's neck, lifting her off the ground as if she weighed nothing.

She swung Kane around, slamming her back into the tiled wall; her hands tightening around Kane's throat.

Kane clutched the girl's wrists; overpowering her wouldn't have been a problem had she been alive, but she had superhuman strength.

Kane brought a foot up, kicking her in the stomach; she loosened her grip but didn't let go.

Kane brought two feet up and kicked, sending her flying backwards.

"Kane?"

Kane ran for the door, but the girl snaked an arm around her neck, stumbling and causing them both to go back into the bathtub.

"Kane, are you okay in there?"

"I'm a little busy here!" She snapped as she tried to loosen the girl's arm which was now choking her.

The door swung open and Moth froze at the sight before him.

Kane let out a choke as the girl vanished.

Moth helped her to her feet, "Are you okay?"

"I just got choked by a psycho charred dead bitch; I'm great."

Moth frowned, "I don't understand why she's haunting you, or why she's trying to kill you."

"She seems jealous. The look she gave me the first time you called was crazy, and then she attacked."

"I'm sorry, London."

He put an arm around her shoulders as they walked out together.

After dinner, Kane went to take a bath; standing at the door for a full five minutes before closing it and taking her shoes off.

She stood in front of the bath, about to undress when she knew all of a sudden that the charred girl was back.

She spun and the girl dived; taking them both into the tub of hot water.

Kane struggled as the ghost stayed put, holding her face firmly under the water.

When she realized the struggling wasn't helping, she blindly reached for the bar of soap, as soon as her hand closed around the soap, she threw it towards the door; satisfied when she heard the loud thud it made.

And then she started struggling again, hoping someone would hear the water and realize something was wrong.

She had just taken in a mouth full of water when the girl vanished and Moth pulled her from the tub.

Gasping and choking for breath she collapsed in a soaking heap on the floor, taking Moth with her.

"That crazy bitch is starting to get on my nerves."

Moth helped her to her feet and waited at the door while she changed before she went to the lounge to wait for him.

Kane was grateful that Alice was asleep and Kelso had gone out because there was no way for them to explain what had just happened.

Moth came in and started throwing blankets and pillows on the floor.

Kane frowned, "What are you doing?"

"You're taking the couch, I'm taking the floor."

"But–"

"No, I don't trust that ghost with you."

Kane was about to protest when she thought back to the ghost, and she nodded.

Moth was right, there was no telling what she would do the

next time she had a chance.

She obviously wanted Kane dead for some reason and Kane had a feeling she wasn't just about to give up.

Kane woke up the next morning to see Moth and his makeshift bed gone.

She got up and went into the kitchen where Alice sat at the counter with coffee.

"Where's Moth?"

"Manners, Kane, good morning."

"Sorry, morning."

"Moth says something attacked you in the bathroom, he didn't tell us what though."

Kane frowned, "So where is he?"

Kelso and Moth walked in.

Moth smiled at her, "Bathroom is sorted."

Kane frowned, "What?"

"You'll see."

She went to the bathroom, the door had been taken off and there was now a railing with a shower curtain around the bath.

Moth came in, stopping next to her, "Now she won't come back in here to attack you."

Kane turned, about to thank him, but froze when she realized how close he was.

They still hadn't discussed their kiss, and she wondered if now was the time to bring it up.

"Moth?"

He moved closer and just as their lips were about to meet, they heard a blood-curdling scream from the kitchen.

Together they ran through to find Alice with a box at her feet,

Kane walked over and gagged, running out the back door; she dropped to her knees and vomited.

She felt Moth rub her back, "London, are you okay?"

The box had a layer of dead rotting birds in it, a picture of her with the words 'YOU'RE NEXT' on it, and a human head.

The eyes that had stared back at her from the box were the same eyes that she saw every morning in the mirror; the head had been her mother's.

"Moth, we need to get Rick here."

He nodded and helped her to her feet.

When Rick showed up ten minutes later it had been Kelso who had called him.

He took their statements and had another officer remove the box before he walked out and sat next to Kane on the grass.

"I'm sorry, that must have been a terrible shock."

Kane nodded.

"Here's my number, call me if you need me, it might take too long if you call the station. I promise you, I will catch this guy."

Kane nodded.

Rick put an arm around her shoulders, "If there's anything you need, let me know."

Moth walked out and cleared his throat.

Rick stood and helped Kane to her feet.

"I better get back to the station. Remember what I said about watching your back."

Moth waited for him to leave before speaking, "What was that about?"

Kane shrugged, "Nothing, guess he's trying to be a good cop."

Moth narrowed his eyes, clearly not believing her.

Kane sighed, "I wish they would just catch him."

"Kay-Kay!"

Kane frowned; there stood Gina and Scott.

Kane's mouth dropped, "What are you doing here?"

Gina rushed forward, wrapping her arms around Kane; ignoring the fact that Kane didn't return the hug.

"I told you I'd come to this dump and visit you."

Kane raised a brow, "It's not that bad."

Gina flipped her long red hair over her shoulder, "It looks rather dead, right, Scotty?" she turned to Scott, who still stood in the doorway, "Scott, come here. What are you standing there for?"

Scott walked over to them looking extremely awkward, giving Kane a small smile and awkward wave.

Kane nodded; she had no intention of being over-friendly with her ex-boyfriend, or her ex-best friend who was now dating her ex-boyfriend.

Scott's eyes fell on Moth.

Kane cleared her throat, "This is Moth. Moth, Gina and Scott."

Gina smirked, "Well, it's nice to meet you Moth. I'm so curious as to why my best friend hasn't mentioned you yet."

"Maybe because we aren't best friends anymore."

Kelso walked out, "Cliff called to check on you, he's on his way over. And I'm going to take Alice to the doctor."

Kane nodded, "Thanks."

Scott waited till Kelso had left before turning to Kane, "What's going on, K?"

Kane ran a hand through her hair and sighed, "Goran."

Scott's eyes bulged, "What? He's here? You need to get out of this place; you can't just sit around while he's after you."

Moth cleared his throat, "She isn't going to run away; she'll be just fine here."

Scott turned to him, "Fine? She'll be fine? In case you haven't noticed, Goran Owens is insane; it's not safe for her to take a risk like this; something could happen to her."

Kane rolled her eyes, "Scott, that's enough; Moth has my back."

"I care about you, Kane!"

"You lost the right to care when we broke up."

Gina stood awkwardly, shooting Scott annoyed glances.

"Kane! Are you okay?"

Cliff came running out, giving her a hug, which she gladly returned.

"I'm good, thanks for coming, Brace Face."

Moth nodded his hellos as Kane introduced Cliff to Gina and Scott.

Gina tilted her head, "So, tell me about this old building you're renovating."

Cliff winced, "An old mental institution."

Gina raised her brows, "Well, that sounds fun. Scott and I will be joining you."

Kane would have protested and told them it wasn't safe, but she stopped herself; Gina could make her own choices, such as dating Scott.

Kane forced a smile, "The more the merrier."

Moth glanced at her with a slight frown but said nothing.

Cliff sighed, "I wish there was a way for us to get out of it."

"What's the big deal?" Asked Gina.

"It's haunted," Cliff went pale as he continued, "The people who go in there don't come back out; one guy came out and he was completely insane."

Gina laughed, "Haunted? And you lot believe it? This place is so lame."

Cliff glared at her, "I do believe it. And you should watch your mouth; you want to piss them off, go ahead, but don't do it around us."

Kane was surprised to see Cliff get so angry; he was so quiet most of the time.

Moth jumped in before the debate could go any further, "Okay, I think that's enough talk about haunting."

Scott nodded, "Yeah, so what is there to do in this place?"

Cliff shrugged, "Not really much."

Gina groaned, "I'm going to die if I have to sit here the whole time."

Kane sighed, "Ice-cream will have to do, Cliff, get the others to meet us there please."

Scott frowned, "K is that really a good idea? I mean, if Goran's around, wouldn't it be safer to stay here?"

Moth pushed past him, "London will be fine; I'll be right there with her."

As Cliff and Kane walked around to the front, he whispered "Looks like we have a bit of an ego contest."

Despite the situation, Kane couldn't help but give a small smile and nod; Cliff was right, there was quite a clash of egos between Moth and Scott.

Scott had always been the type to feel like he had to protect all the women, and that had been one of the reasons they hadn't worked out; Kane had felt like he was a bodyguard more than a boyfriend.

And now with Moth who obviously had taken it upon himself to be the one to keep Kane safe, there was bound to be problems between the two.

Kane could understand Moth's point; something was going on between them and he had every right to care about her well being.

Scott however had no right at all when it came to Kane, and

she planned on getting that message across to him sooner rather than later.

Kane sat in between Cliff and Moth with Gina and Scott opposite them.

Kane turned to Cliff, "When's the rest of us showing up?"

"Collin and Macy will be here in about five minutes, Cassie and Brent should come with them; we can order for them so long."

Gina made a face, "Damn, Kane, you've made friends already."

The waitress appeared and Cliff ordered Bubble-gum ice-cream for Cassie and himself.

Gina ordered rum and raisin.

Kane ordered strawberry for Macy and vanilla for Brent and Collin.

She frowned down at the flavors menu, "I'll have..."

Moth spoke, "Chocolate, right?"

"With caramel." Added Scott.

Moth glared across at him before turning to the waitress, "Two, please"

Kane shot a glare at Scott as the rest of her friends walked in and joined them.

Once the introductions had passed, Kane was feeling a lot better, and decided she wouldn't think of Goran or the asylum; she would enjoy the day with her friends.

Sighing, she lent her head on Moth's shoulder as Macy began talking.

"So, Veda is super pissed off that you took her title."

Gina frowned, "Who is Veda?"

Macy waved her hand in the air, "The Queen Bee at school."

Kane scoffed, "More like queen bitch."

Gina laughed, "Knowing Kane that must have been a show-down; I can just imagine it."

Collin laughed, "Oh yes, Kane gave her some great eye make-up."

Gina shook her head, "That I believe. Her anger issues are still going to land her in deep trouble."

Kane laughed, "G, please, it's already gotten me into deep trouble, on more than one occasion."

Cassie looked nervous, "It can't be so bad, and you're still young."

Gina raised her brows, "Have you seen her file? She's been kicked out of seven schools for violence; jailed for assault twice; jailed for fraud; jailed for unlicensed weapons."

Cassie's eyes went the size of saucers.

Kane cleared her throat, she hadn't minded Cliff and Moth knowing of her past, but she would have preferred for the others not to have found out.

Gina let out a laugh, "Oh, and I forgot the six months in the mental institution."

Kane's eyes snapped up; glaring at Gina.

Moth's arm tightened around her shoulders.

"What for-"

Cliff cut Macy off, "It's none of our business."

Kane cleared her throat, "It was for hearing and seeing things."

Macy's face filled with concern, "Will you be okay in the Misty Asylum?"

Kane nodded, "I'll be fine."

Scott nodded, "And we'll be there to make sure of it."

Moth exhaled loudly.

Cassie shrugged, "Well I'm creeped out about all of this; the sooner we get out of there the better."

Macy nodded, "Especially with all the horror stories of that place."

Gina rolled her eyes, "Don't let some made up scary stories get to you; you can't be scared of myths."

Kane chose to stay quiet; however, the truth was that her time in Misty Meadows had taught her that they were definitely far from myths.

When Moth shifted uncomfortably, she knew he was thinking the same.

Macy frowned, "You don't know this place; it's pretty creepy."

"Creepy? No. Boring; yes." The distaste in Gina's voice was thick; obviously thinking very lowly of the town.

Cliff smiled, "This place just might surprise you."

"I hope so, or I might just die of boredom."

Kane frowned; she and Gina had been so close before, but now sitting with her new friends, she just couldn't understand how she and Gina had ever been friends at all.

Next to her friends, Gina reminded her so much of Veda.

Kane shrugged, "It's really not that bad here; I mean, I'm surviving."

Gina scoffed, "Yeah, but look at how you've changed. You've even toned down a bit."

Macy blinked, "I wouldn't call her toned down; and if she has toned down, I am so glad I didn't know her before!"

Kane couldn't help but laugh at that.

But Gina was right to an extent; she had changed. And she realized at that moment that even though she had hated Misty Meadows at first, she liked it now; it was home.

And she wouldn't change her friends for anything in the

world.

Gina turned to Kane, "You need to get out of school so you can leave this place and come back home."

Kane shrugged, with a smile on her face, "I'm in no rush to leave; I like it here."

She could see Gina wanted to say something but decided against it.

Macy was stressed; she wanted nothing to do with the Asylum, but Kane calmed her, telling her it would all be okay and sounding much more confident than she actually was.

The truth was she had a bad feeling in the pit of her stomach that things were about to take a turn for the worst.

7

Chapter 7

The days went by too fast and before she knew it, they stood outside the Misty Hill Asylum.

Kelso and Brent stood to the side near Veda and her group of airheads.

Mr. Lewis stood in front of the doors, facing them all.

"Good morning, everyone; I'm glad to see you've all made it. Now, you will be in the asylum for the whole holidays; cleaning, painting and fixing. Food and beverages will be provided."

Veda frowned, "Will we be able to keep our phones?"

"Mr. Smith is the supervisor, and he will be the only one with a phone."

Kane's eyes fell to Mr. Smith; Mr. Lewis had sworn he could be trusted to keep everyone safe.

Kane wondered how he would keep them safe; he was a light-haired man in his late thirties, with a very skinny build.

They handed their phones to Mr. Lewis and followed Smith into the asylum.

Kane and Moth were the last to enter, and as the doors closed behind them, she had the feeling of dread in her stomach.

94

The hairs on the back of her neck rose and her blood ran cold as ice.

Let the fun begin

Suddenly, she just knew that not everyone would make it out alive.

Smith turned to them, pulling her from her thoughts, "First of all, call me Zack."

Kane frowned, she wasn't taking interest in anyone at this point; she studied the asylum.

The walls were chipping and the floors were covered in a thick layer of dust and grime; the furniture still stood in its place, also covered in a thick layer of dust.

"How come there haven't been any break-ins?"

Jack frowned, "No one is stupid enough to come in here."

Gina rolled her eyes, "Let me guess, the big bad ghosts?"

She was still laughing when a noise echoed through the asylum; it sounded like metal connecting with a wall somewhere deeper in the building.

Veda jumped, clutching at Kelso's arm, "What the hell was that?"

Kane would have enjoyed the fear in Veda's eyes, had she not been feeling the same way.

Zack smiled, "Nothing to worry about, Veda, it's just the old piping."

Kelso shook Veda off and Kane couldn't help but smile at that.

Gina shook her head, "You people are crazy."

Zack started explaining how they could all sleep in the main lounge area, or choose to separate from the group at night, as long as they all stayed on the same floor and got up early the next morning for work to begin.

They all decided for night one, staying together would be best, so sleeping bags were spread out on the floor.

While everyone talked and joked, Kane's attention was on the doorway that led out to the long hallway.

'Come'

Kane frowned; that was a female voice, a voice she didn't recognize.

'Come'

Kane stood, "I'll be right back."

Zack turned, "I'm not sure if all the lights work."

Kane picked up a camping lamp, "I'll take this with."

Moth stood, "Let me go with you."

'Come Alone'

Kane shook her head, "No worries, I'm just going to the toilet, I won't be long."

She walked out quickly, vaguely hearing Veda saying that she was crazy for walking off alone.

Kane frowned when she realized that the passageway and all the doorways leading off it were in complete darkness.

She sighed, "You were in jail, you can't be afraid of a little darkness."

She started forward with the lamp held out in front of her.

She stopped dead when she realized she had gone so far down the passage that she could no longer see the light from the lounge area.

The door to her right caught her attention, she wasn't sure why, but she felt that she needed to go in.

Pushing the door open and going in, she was met with an office.

Going in, she set the lamp on the corner of the desk and opened one of the drawers; it held a stack of files.

Pulling them out, she set them on the desk and took the first one; opening it she found a picture and details such as names, height, address and illness.

She sighed and reached for the lamp, about to leave when a sudden gust of wind blew through, sending a few files from the desk.

She picked the files up, and as she was about to place them back on the stack, she froze at the name on the corner of the file which she had just been about to cover.

Star.

She dropped the files and opened the file with the name Star on it.

The picture was of a man with long brown hair and eyes identical to Moths.

The name was Jethro Star.

She carried on reading the file, realizing that he was Moth's father and that he had been released around the same time Moth had been born.

She went through the file quickly, scanning the pages, and taking note that they said he was an extremely violent man.

Kane frowned, trying to figure out why she had been led to this.

As if in answer, the second drawer slid open.

She picked up the first file and opened it; it was a file on one of the nurses who had worked in the asylum; she had been fired for having a relationship with a patient; Jethro Star.

The name listed was Jasmine Hashmi.

Kane realized this woman must have been Moth's mother; her hand going to the pendant around her neck.

'Keep away from him. Break the Curse'

She returned the files, took the lamp and walked out, closing the door behind her.

She turned, planning on returning to the lounge area where the others were, but suddenly she froze; fear gripping her.

She had an intense feeling that someone was behind her.

Gripping the lamp tightly, she turned; every bit of her body screamed at her to run.

Instead, she took a step forward.

There was something wet on the floor, and she stepped closer to examine it.

Water trickled down from the floor above; Kane was just about to reach for it when she heard the loud clanging sound again and decided it would be best to get out of there.

She turned and heading back towards the lounge, her head whipping around to make sure no one was behind her; she walked straight into someone.

She let out a gasp, ready to attack; but relaxed when she realized it was Moth.

He frowned, "Where were you? Are you okay?"

Kane nodded, "I came across an office with all these files in it; was your father Jethro Star?"

Moth's frown deepened, "How do you?"

"He was a patient here, released in the same year that you were born."

"What? I had no idea."

"Was your mother Jasmine Hashmi?"

Moth's eyes widened, "Yes."

"She was a nurse here; fired for having a relationship with your father while he was still a patient."

Moth frowned again, "How did you find all of this out?"

Kane shrugged, "I followed clues."

"Another spirit?"

Kane nodded; grateful that he didn't think she was crazy.

He sighed and held out his hand to her, "Let's get back before they come looking for us."

Together they walked back into the lounge, as they passed Veda, Kane heard her muttering "Freaks."

Kane stopped and turned, "Do you have something to say, Veda?"

Zack looked up, "Girls."

Veda grinned smugly and Kane took another step towards her but Moth squeezed her hand and she turned away, walking with him to the now cleaned couch near Cassie, Cliff, Collin and Macy.

Gina and Scott were in the middle of the room, with everyone else scattered around.

Kane got onto the couch, feeling as if things were about to start getting a lot stranger in the asylum.

She fell asleep with the thought of dread in her mind, and her hand entwined with

8

Chapter 8

The day started rather normally.

They were busy in one of the large dining rooms; painting the walls.

Veda turned to Kane, "I need the ladder."

Kane rolled her eyes, "So go get it."

Veda stormed towards the ladder, purposefully kicking over a tin of white paint, and sending a large blob onto Macy's dark jeans.

Kane narrowed her eyes, "Watch it, Veda."

Aside from Cliff and Collin, the room was just the girls; the guys had gone with Zack to take care of the plumbing in one of the bathrooms.

Veda glared at Kane, "Or what?"

Kane had been crouching at the wall, she stood, "Don't push me, Veda."

Gina cleared her throat, "K, let it go."

Kane ignored her and continued her stare down with Veda.

Veda smiled, suddenly ripping Cliff's glasses from his face, she threw them to the floor and stood on them.

Cliff glared at her, "You're such a bitch."

Veda rolled her eyes, "Shut up, four eyes."

"Veda," Kane started towards her, "You just never learn, do you?" she picked up a half-full tin of paint by the handle as she reached Veda.

Kane smiled, and swung the tin, making a satisfying sound as it connected with the side of Veda's face; sending her spinning before she hit the ground.

Gina glared at Kane and crouched next to Veda, checking to see if she was okay.

"Girls?"

Kane turned to Zack, "She deserved it, I swear."

Zack sighed, "What happened?"

Veda sat up, her face already a dark purple with a bit of blood seeping through.

Gina stood, "Kane, you can't-"

Kane spun, "You stay the hell out of this. That little bitch and her airhead friends have been giving Cliff and Macy a hard time their whole lives; as their friend, I refuse to allow it! That's what friends do, Gina, not that you would know anything about that, because not only did you jump to get my leftovers the moment I left, you're also just like Veda."

Zack held up his hands, "Girls, please."

Kane spun to him, "Take this as a lesson; don't leave us in the same room together again." She dropped the tin and walked out.

She was surprised to see that Zack followed her.

"Kane, I'd like to speak to you for a second. This whole thing is for you and Veda to learn to at least be civil to each other, and for you to stop being so violent."

"She broke Cliff's glasses, so you might want to have this

chat with her. Keep her in check." She turned and walked away from him.

Taking a few turns, she came to the rooms.

Most of the doors were broken, so she went into one of the rooms, frowning when her eyes landed on the restraints on the walls and bed.

She knew from personal experience about the restraints on the bed; she thought back to the first few days in the mental institution, she had been tied to the bed herself, they had said she was too much of a risk to have her loose, she had spent so much time tied to the bed, in and out of consciousness.

She shook her head, ridding herself of the terrible memories.

She turned to walk out, but the door slammed shut, she slowly walked up to the door and tried the handle, even as she did, she knew it wouldn't work.

Sighing, she turned and slid down to the floor, her back against the door.

Suddenly she heard a dripping sound, and she snapped her head up; there was a thin line of rusty water running down the wall from the ceiling.

Getting to her feet, she went over to take a closer look at the deep red water.

She rolled her eyes, "Bloodied water, how original."

As she turned to go back to the door, her hand grazed along the bed.

The moment her hand touched the bed the restraints curled around her wrist, tightening like a second skin.

She hysterically tried to get her hand free, the memories that feeling brought back making the panic even worse.

Suddenly she stopped her thrashing as the old, dusty sheet rose up above her.

"No, no, no."

The sheet came down, covering her; wrapping tightly around her.

She gasped as she was thrown face-first onto the bed, something pushing her face into the mattress, suffocating her.

She could feel herself getting light-headed; her one wrist still tied to the bed.

She threw herself to the side, tipping the bed over onto her.

The heavy steel frame felt as if it was crushing her chest.

She was battling to get air in and her face started to tingle as she struggled against the bed.

Her vision started going as she heard the door open, the bed was pulled off her and she saw Moth.

"London, are you okay?" He dropped to her side, worry filling his face.

Kane nodded, happy that she could breathe again.

"What happened?"

Kane sat up slowly, "The door closed and locked me in, the restraints on the bed closed around my wrist, and something tried to suffocate me."

Moth frowned, "What? That's it; you're not to go anywhere alone."

Suddenly Zack was in the doorway, "What the hell happened?"

Moth all but shouted the events at Zack, "We have to get out of here; she could have been killed."

Zack scanned the room before turning to Kane, "Are you okay?"

Kane was almost one hundred percent sure he looked disappointed as if he had expected something more to have happened.

She nodded, "I'm fine."

9

Chapter 9

Moth stood and helped her to her feet.

Zack was about to speak when they heard a blood-curdling scream from somewhere in the asylum.

The three of them ran from the room, heading down the passage and into the dining hall.

Layla was on the floor clutching her hand.

Zack helped Layla to her feet, her hand pouring with blood.

Kane's eyes were on the puddle of blood at Layla's feet which only seems to grow.

Zack frowned, "Layla, what happened?"

She shook her head, "I don't know," she shook her head again, "It was like I was being pulled in here, and when I got in... I don't remember, it was like I passed out I guess and when I woke up my hand was full of blood."

Zack was busy wrapping his shirt around Layla's hand.

Kane frowned, this was starting to be a clear sign that the spirits were not interested in playing; she turned to Moth and knew he thought the same.

Moth cleared his throat, "Zack, we need to get out of this

place, before anything worse happens."

Zack sighed, "Let's just get Layla fixed up first."

They headed for the door, but Kane stated, "I'll clean up in her."

Zack nodded as he ushered Layla from the room.

She waited until she was sure they were gone before turning to Moth, "Something pulling her in here; this is happening faster than I thought it would."

Moth nodded, "I know; we need to get everyone out of here and fast."

Kane turned slightly, just in time to see a wooden chair fly into the air and come whizzing towards them.

She dropped to the floor just as the chair passed, slamming into the wall and shattering.

Kane raised her brows, "Looks like something doesn't want us to leave."

He held out his hand, "Let's go."

He helped her up and together they went to the lounge area.

Cliff, Collin, Kelso and Macy came to them immediately.

Kane scanned the room.

Zack was crouched in front of Layla while she leaned against Jack on the couch; Mac stood in the corner with his arms around a worried-looking Stacey; Brent and Scott stood near the fireplace; Veda sat with her knees pulled up to her chest, arms wrapped around her legs; And Gina stood at the back of the couch with her hand resting on Layla's shoulder.

Kelso frowned, "What happened?"

Moth started explaining and Kane's eyes wandered to the clock on the table.

"It's not midnight."

"London?" Moth was staring at her with a worried look on

his face.

She realized that everyone was staring at her.

She motioned to the clock, "It says it's midnight when it isn't."

Kelso checked his watch, "My watch says midnight."

Brent nodded, "Yeah, so does mine."

Collin frowned, "Same here."

Scott turned, "Here too."

Mac nodded, "Same."

"So does mine." Said Stacey.

Moth turned to Zack, "We need to leave."

"Just relax."

Kelso took a step forward, "No, we need to leave."

The fireplace suddenly popped and flames shot up, sending Brent and Scott diving away from it.

Zack's mouth dropped.

Moth spun, "Now do you believe we need to leave?"

'You won't get out'

Kane shook her head, panic filling her body, "It won't let us leave."

Brent frowned, "Call Lewis if we can't get out."

While Kelso and Moth took the keys from Zack to unlock the doors, Zack started searching for a phone with a signal, and Kane took a crowbar to the windows.

Kelso and Moth returned, Moth threw the keys against the wall.

Zack sighed, "There's no signal here."

Kane sighed, the windows weren't breaking; she sat on the floor, dropping the crowbar to her side.

Stacey started pacing, "We'll get out of here."

Zack stood, "Brent, Kelso and Moth, go down to the basement, the electrical box is down there, do what you can, we need proper lights in this place."

Brent and Kelso nodded and walked out, but Moth came over to Kane.

"London, you don't move from this room until I'm back."

She nodded, "Just make sure you stay safe."

He nodded, before kissing her and walking out.

Kane lent her head against the wall, and closed her eyes, having Moth around made her feel so much better.

'Stick Together'

Kane's eyes flew open at the sound of the woman's voice.

"Where's Stacey?"

Zack shrugged, "She went to get food."

Kane stood, "I'll help her."

Walking down the passage, she wondered why they would let Stacey walk around alone, especially at a time like this.

She opened the door to the room where they had been keeping the food in and frowned; there was no sign of Stacey.

"Stacey?"

Kane scanned the room, freezing at the sight of blood on the floor in front of the cupboard.

She ran to the cupboard and pulled the doors open; tumbling to the floor as Stacey's bloodied corpse fell on top of her.

"Moth! Zack! Get in here!"

She shoved the body off and got to her feet.

Zack ran in, "What... Oh my God."

"I came in, and saw the blood on the floor, and when I checked the cupboard, she fell out."

Zack let out a shaky breath, "Go back to the others, I'll clean this up. And no one leaves that room until I'm back."

Kane nodded and walked out, going back to the lounge and

stopping in the doorway.

Moth and the others weren't back yet.

Veda was the first to look up, "Oh God."

This had everyone turning.

"We need to wait for for-"

Veda's voice shook, "Why is there blood on your clothes?"

Kane glanced down suddenly, she had forgotten about that, "Um, I'm sorry guys. I found Stacey."

Mac fell to his knees, burying his face in his hands.

Veda had tears streaming down her face, "Is she? Is she gone?"

Kane nodded silently.

Macy stood with her back against Collin, looking terrified; Cassie was on her knees with an arm around Mac who sobbed on his knees; Jack sat with his arm tightly around Layla; Scott and Gina stood behind Veda.

Cliff came up to Kane and put an arm around her shoulders, "I'm sorry you had to find her."

"I just want to get out of here."

The lights flickered on and Kane breathed a sigh of relief; Moth would be back soon.

Cliff smiled, "We will get out of here."

Kane nodded even though she didn't believe that.

Brent and Kelso returned with Moth who frowned at Kane's appearance.

"London, what happened?"

Veda let out a shriek, "We're all going to die."

Brent scanned the room, "Where's Stacey?"

Kane sighed, "I found her in the cupboard. I don't know what happened."

Moth wrapped an arm around her, "We're going to be fine. I

will make sure you get out of here, even if it's the last thing I do."

Kane kept her mouth shut; she had no idea what to believe anymore.

Zack came in, "At least there's light. Okay, listen, something is happening here, obviously; I don't know what, but something is definitely not right. We stick together in groups."

Veda stood, "I can't do this, and we can't just stay here; break a door or something."

Kane sighed, "If that were a possibility, we would have done it already."

Gina stood and made her way to the doorway.

Kane blocked her, "Where do you think you're going?"

Gina rolled her eyes, "I need the toilet."

Kane picked up the crowbar, "Girls, who else needs a toilet break?"

Macy and Veda walked over

10

Chapter 10

They walked out behind Kane, with Moth walking behind them.

Kane walked into the bathroom first, Moth standing at the door to make sure she was safe, as well as those in the passage.

Kane sat on one of the rows of sinks when the others came in, Moth still keeping an eye on the passage.

Suddenly, Kane felt uneasy with her backs to the mirrors and she got to her feet, turning to face them.

Her eyes went wide and she took a step back.

The reflection that stared back at her was the bathroom, but the difference was that in the mirror, it was a murder scene; the walls and floor covered in blood.

One of the stall doors opened and Veda walked out.

"What's wrong with you?"

Kane shook her head, expecting the scene before her to change, but it didn't; it still showed the bloodied bathroom.

"You look as if the mirror is about to attack you."

Kane turned to her, "If you're done, get out."

Veda rolled her eyes and walked out, Kane was sure she had muttered 'freak', but she figured now was not the time to be concerned about that.

Gina and Macy walked out of their stalls, washed their hands and left the bathroom.

Kane was about to follow when she noticed the trickle of red water running down one of the walls, she was drawn to it, but as she went toward it Moth called and she walked out.

Moth stayed close to her as they walked towards the lounge.

As they were about to follow the others in, he caught her arm, "London, what happened?"

Kane sighed and explained what she had seen in the mirror and how she kept seeing bloodied water that she seemed drawn to.

Moth ran a hand through his hair, "It's the spirits; they're trying to mess with you."

Kane nodded, knowing he was right.

"I'm going to speak to Zack, you need to go get cleaned up and out of those clothes, and I'm not letting you go alone."

Kane nodded, only realizing then that she was still in the clothes that were covered in Stacey's blood.

She waited at the door while Moth went and spoke to Zack.

He returned at took the crowbar from her, "Get a change of clothes and let's go."

After getting light blue jeans and a light blue spaghetti strapped top with a pair of her black combat boots, they went to the showers.

Moth placed his hands on her shoulders, "London, I want you to know that I will make sure you get out of this, alive. But if I don't…"

Kane lent forward and kissed him, "Moth, we will have all the time in the world to talk once we get out of here."

She turned and went into one of the showers, pulling the

curtain closed and getting undressed.

She couldn't lose hope, and she wouldn't allow Moth to either.

She stood under the warm water, watching as it turned red as it washed Stacey's blood from her body.

She scrubbed herself before switching the water off and sticking her hand out of the curtain, "Towel."

Moth handed her a towel and she dried before he passed her the clothes; she felt a slight twinge of shyness when she realized he had probably seen the underwear she would be wearing.

Getting dressed, she walked out and sat next to him on the bench while she put her boots on.

"Moth, are you okay?" She asked as she tied her hair into a messy ponytail.

He nodded, "Yes. Are you?"

Kane nodded, "Yeah; we need to figure out how to get out of here."

"Yeah; and fast by the looks of things."

Kane nodded, not sure of what else she could do; she couldn't tell him she thought they would all die in the asylum.

He took her hand in his and looked her in the eyes, "London, I think I've fallen in love with you, and when we get out of here, I'd really like it if you would give me the chance to be the guy you see me as."

Despite the situation, Kane smiled and kissed him softly, "I would love that."

They got up and went back to the lounge; Kane had a little more hope in her, she now had something to look forward to when they got out of the asylum.

'One in the closet, one in the air.'

Kane frowned and looked up, but saw nothing.

She looked around and noticed someone was missing.

"Where's Mac?"

Suddenly everyone was looking around.

Zack stood, "He must have snuck out when I wasn't paying attention."

Kane turned, "We have to find him. Now."

"Moth, come with me. Brent and Kelso, keep everyone here." Zack headed for the door.

Kane went to follow, but Zack blocked her, "Where do you think you're going?"

She rolled her eyes and pushed past him, not caring if he didn't want her going with; she needed to find Mac.

Moth and Zack followed, neither very happy with the fact that Kane was with them.

'One in the closet.'

Kane frowned as they passed the room where she had found Stacey.

Moth and Zack started calling for Mac.

'A dead man can't hear your calls, you fools.'

Kane froze; her blood turning to ice as she got a brief picture in her mind of the dining hall where Layla had been.

Every door they passed was opened and inspected; Kane continued towards the dining hall, knowing that would be where they found him.

'One in the air.'

Kane stopped, "Guys! It's Mac."

When Moth and Zack ran in they both stopped dead in their tracks; their eyes on Mac's lifeless body hanging from a wire wrapped around his neck.

Moth and Zack lifted the body and Kane stood on a chair to undo the wire around his neck, the whole while trying to ignore his lifeless stare.

She climbed down from the chair, watching as Zack felt for a pulse, she knew he wouldn't find one; they were too late.

Zack shook his head, "He's gone."

'Two down.'

Kane sighed, "Two people are dead; we need to get out of here."

Zack shook his head sadly, "Kane, the doors are unbreakable; the windows are barred; there's no cell phone signal; there is no way out."

'Basement.'

Kane frowned, that was the female voice again.

"Is there a basement?"

Zack frowned, "Yes, but it's not just around the corner, this place is huge."

Moth nodded, "Yeah, there's a small room downstairs where the electrical box is, but it's walled off from the rest of the basement."

Kane had a strong feeling that they couldn't trust Zack.

'Trust no-one.'

"Okay, let's get to that basement."

Zack nodded, "Get the others while I move the body."

'Leave the body.'

Kane shook her head, "Leave the body; getting to the basement is the most important right now."

Zack stood, "Are you forgetting who's in charge here?"

"With you in charge, two people are dead. We're not doing things your way anymore." She headed for the door and Moth waited for Zack to walk out before following.

They walked into the lounge and Veda stood, "He's dead, isn't he?"

Kane nodded, "Yes. We can't just sit around and wait for

someone to find us; everyone grabs something that can be used as a weapon." She picked up the crowbar and held it tightly in her hands.

Scott came over to her, "K, what exactly is the plan?"

"Find the basement."

Zack turned, "And then what?"

"I don't know yet."

Zack lowered his voice, "You don't know? You want to lead us into the basement without an actual plan?"

Moth came closer, "Well, it's better than sitting here and doing nothing."

"Is it really? How do we know we aren't getting led into worse?"

Kane stepped back, "You can stay here and be picked off, or you can come with me." She walked out, and soon everyone followed.

Cassie frowned, "So what now?"

"Okay, I'll walk up here; Moth stay in the back, Scott right; Brent, left. That way everyone in the middle is barricaded and safe."

Zack stepped forward, "I am still in charge here, Kane; Mr. Lewis put me in charge."

Kane narrowed her eyes at him, "Those rules went out the window the moment I found Stacey dead, on your watch."

Kelso frowned and came over to them, "Let's start moving, people. Kane, take up the back with Moth, I'll walk up here, and Zack will join me and give the directions." Kelso gripped the back of Zack's neck and firmly pulled him along.

As the group moved forward, Kane fell in step with Moth.

"Why am I walking back here instead of upfront?"

"Because from here you can keep an eye on Zack, because the

rest can't hear what we talk about, and lastly because the closer you are to me, the better it is for me to make sure you're safe," he frowned, "Are you okay?"

Kane nodded, "Yeah, I just go this weird tingling feeling when we passed that room."

It was the room she had found Stacey in.

Moth nodded, "Okay, well, stay close, we don't know how long this is going to take; this place is huge."

'Slowly.'

It was the woman's helpful voice again.

Kane cleared her voice and spoke so they could all hear her, "Slowly; be on the lookout, be alert."

11

Chapter 11

"There's writing on the wall."

Kane and Moth pushed their way to the front where Kelso stood.

Zack waved a hand in the air, "It's just scribbling."

Kane frowned and set her hand against the wall, her body buzzed with electricity and even though she had never seen it before, she knew what language it was.

"It's Enochian." She tilted her head, and as she stared at the writing, the message flashed before her eyes.

"No one move, it says only those with a light step may-"

Kane was cut off by Layla's scream as the floor separated, leaving a large gap, too wide to jump across.

As Jack grabbed a hold of Layla's hand to pull her up, he yelped and dived back, letting go of her.

Kane dived, landing on her stomach just in time to grab a hold of Layla's wrist; she saw why Jack had left her.

Layla screamed and wriggled in pain; at the bottom of the hole was a sea of deformed bony hands grasping at Layla's ankles, their faces almost skeleton, dirty bloodied and bruised.

Tears and mascara streamed down Layla's face as she looked up at Kane with pleading eyes, "Please, don't drop me."

Kane thought of all the time Layla had been horrible to Cliff and Macy, and she briefly considered dropping her.

But she felt Moth hold onto her and she reached down with her free hand and grabbed a hold of Layla.

With Moth's help, she pulled Layla to safety, shocked to see bloodied gashes on her ankles where the ghosts and been grabbing.

Kelso crouched in front of her, "Are you okay?"

Layla nodded, then shook her head, wrapped her arms around Kelso and sobbed.

Veda turned to Kane, "What now?"

With a heavy sigh, Kane stood, " We cross."

Gina frowned, "Are you crazy? We can't walk on the air."

"We're going to walk over that bit of floor still left against the wall," she said as she walked over to the hole, "Come on."

"That floor is hardly there! It's a few inches across, at most." Veda's voice was shrill with panic.

Kane sighed, "There's no other way; Kelso, you first."

Kelso didn't argue; he started off wobbling and Kane held her breath until he was safely across.

Kane shoved Zack forward, "Go."

"I really think we should–"

Kane cut him off, "Walk, Zack."

He started off slowly and Moth came over to Kane.

"I don't like this, London, what if you fall?"

Kane didn't respond; they all knew what would happen if one of them fell.

Once Zack was across and being kept firmly in place by Kelso, Kane turned, "Macy, go."

Macy let out an extremely shaky breath before taking a few steps forward.

She took another step, looked down and gasped; starting to sway back and forth, she tried to clutch the walls as tears escaped her eyes.

Collin tried to rush forward but Moth held him in place; knowing that he would only end up taking them both down.

Kane forced her voice to stay calm as she spoke, "Mace, breathe. You need to stay calm and stop looking down, they can't hurt you. Come on, Mace, you can do this, just keep your eyes on safety and go for it."

Macy took two more steps, and once again paused.

"Macy, dammit, move!" Kane gasped as Macy speed walked across, as she reached the end, she started falling over, but Kelso grabbed a hold of her and pulled her to safety.

Kane let out the breath she had been holding, she felt sick to her stomach and tried to swallow the lump that had formed in her throat.

Moth put an arm around her, "London, are you okay? Look, she's okay."

Kane nodded, "Cass, you're up."

Cassie nodded and started across.

Kane frowned, "Don't look down, Cass."

Cassie took a deep breath and carried on; making it safely across.

"Veda, go."

Veda rolled her eyes and headed across.

Gina came over to them, "Kane, what's going on here?"

Kane kept her eyes on the others across from them, "We told you it's haunted," she motioned for Layla to go.

Layla was sobbing, shaking mess as she started across.

"Layla; calm, be calm and focus on safety."

Gina turned to Kane, "Hearing you tell people to stay calm is so odd."

Kane's eyes went to the bottom of the dark hole, "As you said, I've changed," The spirits at the bottom of the hole weren't showing themselves, but Kane knew they were still there, patiently waiting to make their move and attack.

Moth nodded at Gina, "Go."

She didn't need to be told twice, starting towards safety instantly.

"You're next, London."

Kane shook her head, "No, I'm last."

"London..."

Kane ignored him, her eyes on Jack as he went across.

Scott came to them, "K, you should get across."

She ignored his words, "Scott, you can go."

Scott turned, "Collin, go."

Again, Kane held her breath until Collin was safe across and in Macy's arms.

Cliff frowned, "K, without my glasses everything is really blurry."

Kane turned from where Brent was walking across, 'Cliff, you don't need to see, just stay calm and keep one foot in front of the other. You will make it across." She knew her voice sounded a lot more confident than she actually felt.

Cliff gave her a small smile before he nervously took a step towards safety.

Kane couldn't breathe as she watched her closest friend blindly battle to cross, she wanted to say something encouraging, but with the lump lodged in her throat, she knew her voice would betray her.

Moth tightened his arm around her, "He'll make it."

Kane let out a sigh of relief and sagged against Moth as Cliff made it to safety.

Moth removed his arm and nudged her gently, "London, it's your turn."

She nodded; she knew he and Scott wouldn't allow her to go last.

As she took the first few steps, she realized that it was a lot harder than she had thought.

Halfway across and she stopped, her eyes going down to the black pit as the spirits revealed themselves once again, hands outstretched towards her.

"London, eyes up."

She could hear Moth, but she couldn't take her eyes from them.

'Come to us'

"London!"

'Save them, come to us'

It was as if their voices were pulling her.

"Dammit, London! I love you and I will not lose you like this; get across or I'm jumping in."

Kane snapped out of her trance at Moths words, he loved her? Not thought he was falling in love with her.

Looking up, she hurried across; Kelso helping her the last bit.

Cliff was the first to wrap his arms around her.

"You had us worried there, K."

Kane lowered her voice, "They spoke to me, and called me to go to them."

Macy frowned, "What?"

Kane turned, Scott was already safe, Moth was starting across now.

The moment Moth's feet touched safety Kane was in his arms.

"London, what happened back there? It looked like I was about to lose you," he pulled back slightly to look at her.

"They called to me."

Zack cleared his throat, "Can we get going?"

Without another word, the group started walking.

Moth turned to her, "What did they say?"

Kane shook her head, "I'll tell you later."

They passed an infirmary, and Kane stopped.

"Wait, we should clean those cuts on Layla."

She went in and Layla followed close behind.

Kane turned the light on and it flickered a few times before coming on.

Kane threw Layla a bandage and gauze, "Put that on," she opened the first aid kit and found it empty.

The woman's voice told her to fill it, so she did.

Layla was still busy with her ankles so Kane went over to lean against the wall; stopping when she noticed that there was a newer mark on the wall, obviously newer than the other marks.

Kane lent forward and placed her hand against it, regretting it immediately.

The room changed into something no longer deserted, clean walls, and Layla was no longer on the floor.

Instead, there was a doctor at a desk, a female nurse standing in front of him.

"We must finish the testing."

"Doctor, we can't; things are going wrong. The test subjects are showing signs of complete brutality."

"I am on the brink of a breakthrough, here. So we lose a few lives, so what? It is more than worth it."

Kane jumped up from the floor, the room was back to normal;

Moth sitting almost over her, face filled with worry.

"What happened, London?"

"The doctor was using the patients for his experiment; it was causing them to become more brutal."

"London, that's terrible, but don't do that again; we didn't know what was going on, your eyes were snow white. God, you scared me."

Kane stood and hugged him, "I'm okay."

They walked out and Kane motioned for them to continue walking.

"Left or right?" Asked Kelso.

Kane frowned, "I thought Zack was-"

'Left'

"Left; we go left."

Zack shook his head, "No, we go right."

"I agree." Jack went right, and as Zack was about to follow, a door dropped down, separating them from Jack.

"Help me!"

Kane went to the door, "Jack, calm down, we just need to figure out how to open the door."

"No, no, get away from me. Kane, help me, there's something coming towards me!" His voice sounded hysterical.

"What is coming towards you?"

Suddenly they were met with screams, gurgling and bones crunching.

Kane stepped away from the door as blood seeped from it.

The door slowly started rolling up.

"Kelso, get Mace and Layla away from here."

The door opened to reveal a large puddle of blood and what was left of Jack.

His legs mangled and his throat a gaping hole.

Kane turned, "Let's go."

No one argued and they headed left.

When they reached the others, Layla turned.

"Where's Jack."

Kane shook her head and looked away as Layla started to cry and Kelso put an arm around her.

They had been walking for a few minutes when Kelso asked that they take a rest for Layla.

They found a second dining hall and went in.

Kane stood near the door with her back against the wall as everyone else found a place to sit.

Layla was sobbing in Kelso's arms; Cassie, Cliff, Collin and Macy sat close together; Brent, Gina and Scott sat near the door; and Moth sat next to Kane's legs.

Kane's eyes were on Veda, who was pacing as if in some sort of trance.

"London, sit down, you also need rest."

Kane shook her head, still not taking her eyes from Veda, she had a strong feeling that she needed to keep her eyes on Veda.

Moth stood, "London, I might not make it out of here–"

Kane spun towards him, "Don't you dare say that."

"London, come on, these things are picking us off; I told you I would get you out safely, and I will, I'm just saying, I might not be able to get myself out," he took hold of one of her hands, "What I said back there, I meant it."

"Moth, shut up; everything you're saying is just sounding like a goodbye."

Moth sighed, "London, I just need you to know that I love you."

Kane cleared her throat, "I love you too, but that doesn't mean you can go and get yourself killed."

Moth lent forward, but as their lips were about to meet, there was a scream and they turned to see that Veda had fallen halfway through the floor.

Kane was the first to get to her, pulling Veda out, ignoring her screams as the broken bits of wood cut into her thighs.

She wrapped her arms around Kane, "Thank you."

Kane nodded and went towards the door, "Come on, we can't sit around."

As soon as they were walking again Kane got the feeling there was still a lot that was going to go wrong.

Moth took her free hand, "You sure there's going to be a way out in the basement?"

Kane shook her head, "It just feels right."

Moth sighed, "London, I need to tell you something."

"What the hell is that?" Screamed Cassie.

Everyone turned to where Cassie stood frozen with a look of fear on her face as she stared ahead at an empty space.

Kane dropped Moth's hand and went over to Cassie, "What do you see, Cass?"

"She's," Cassie took a step back, "She's screaming, make her stop; she looks rotten." She took another step back, pulling Kane in front of her like a shield.

Kane frowned, "Cassie, I don't see anything," Kane took a step back suddenly, "Crap, I see her."

The woman had hair that mattered to the sides of her face, eyes almost hollow, rotting almost pitch black skin, broken bleeding teeth, her mouth twisted in a silent scream.

Veda frowned, "What is it?"

"Cass, can you hear it?"

Cassie nodded, "Yes."

Zack came forward, "Who?"

Cliff sighed, "My guess is that it's Screaming Sally."

Brent nodded, "They say if you hear her, she marks you for death."

Instantly, Cassie dropped to the floor, sobbing.

Cliff ran to Cassie's side.

Kane didn't take her eyes from the ghost of Screaming Sally.

Kane narrowed her eyes, and in a moment of complete insanity, she hissed at the ghost; completely aware of how crazy she must have looked to her friends.

The ghost's mouth shut and she tilted her head to the side as she stared at Kane in confusion.

"London, what the hell are you doing?"

Kane shrugged, "Pissing off a ghost."

Gina raised her brows, "Are you crazy?"

Kane smiled, not taking her eyes from the spirit, "Of course." She tightened her grip on the crowbar, "Cliff, get Cassie up. The rest of you give me some space."

"London." Moth's voice held a warning in it.

"I just want to try something." She waited until the others had moved back, "Now scream, bitch." She swung the crowbar, surprisingly connecting with the ghost's head, making a sick wet sound as the ghost went into the wall before disappearing.

"Now let's get out of here before she decides to cash in on Cassie."

No one needed to be told twice, and everyone started moving.

12

Chapter 12

'Look'

Kane frowned; her eyes darting in all areas as they walked.

'Look'

Kane's blood turned cold as her eyes landed on the small homemade bracelet lying against a door they had passed.

The bracelet with the letters 'G.K' engraved into it.

The bracelet Goran had made.

"London, what's wrong?"

Kane shook her head, "Nothing." She knew if Moth knew that Goran was in the asylum, he would be set on finding him, and she couldn't risk that.

Zack stopped and motioned to a door, "It's down there."

Kane stepped forward and took the door handle, suddenly having a brief flashback to the doctor throwing a body down the steps.

Sighing, she opened the door to reveal a long set of steps disappearing down into darkness.

Zack took a step back, "I'm not going down first."

Kane rolled her eyes and stormed down, ignoring Moth's complaints as he followed her.

The moment she stepped off the last step, her feet landed in the water.

Feeling along the wall for the light switch, she switched the lights on; the basement floor was covered in water from the leaking pipes.

The others came down the steps; Kelso and Zack being last.

"So where's the big exit, Kane?" Zack smirked snidely.

Kane scanned the bare room; there weren't even any windows, yet she somehow knew that the female voice had not let her down, "It's here somewhere."

He threw his arms in the air and turned in a slow circle, "Where? Is it invisible? Or maybe you're seeing things again?" he dropped his arms and took a few steps closer to her, "You sent us on a wild goose chase for nothing."

Kane narrowed her eyes, about to reply when they heard they heard the door slam shut, which was the exact moment that Moth tackled Zack to the floor, throwing punches at him.

Brent took off up the stairs while Kelso and Scott pulled Moth off of Zack.

Zack stood and Moth glared at him, "Don't you ever even think of getting aggressive with her again, or I swear, you will be left dead."

Kane put a hand on his shoulder, in the hopes of calming him down.

Brent charged back down the stairs, "It's locked."

Kane sighed, "Of course it is. Just give me a second to figure the place out, I'll find the exit."

Zack was pacing, "You got Jack killed. You are responsible for all the attacks."

Veda rolled her eyes, "Don't be stupid, she's the one who helped me, and she's the one who has been trying to help all of us," she shrugged, "Shut up and let her get us out of here."

Kane had never thought she would see the day where Veda actually stood up for her.

Kane scanned the room, studying every bit of the room as she slowly walked around it.

'More will die.'

Kane froze; it was the female voice, warning her.

Kane had a terrible feeling in her stomach as she turned slowly to see Screaming Sally pointing at Cassie.

Cassie screamed, jumped and ran to the wall, where she smashed her head against it.

Kane tackled Cassie to the floor as the others took a few steps back from Cassie whose head was pouring with blood while she thrashed wildly.

Cliff ran over, holding Cassie down as Kane jumped to her feet and went towards the ghost with the crowbar.

Kane swung but Screaming Sally grabbed a hold of the crow-bar and punched Kane in the face, literally sending her flying across the room where she dropped into the dirty water.

She was quick to get to her feet, running and tackling Screaming Sally just as she reached over Cassie, who was still screaming and thrashing uncontrollably.

Sitting over the spirit, Kane began punching her, ignoring the ache in her own jaw from where Screaming Sally had punched her.

Screaming Sally lent forward, her hand gripping Kane's thigh and she instantly felt a searing pain, she tried to get the ghost's hand off here and Screaming Sally threw Kane off of her; diving over to place a finger against Cassie's head.

Kane tried to get to her feet, but the burn on her thigh was too painful; it had burned clean through her jeans and left a raw scorched patch in her skin.

Cassie let out an agonizing scream before blood began pouring from her mouth and she went limp in Cliff's arms.

Kane pulled herself over through the water, wrapping an arm around Cliff.

"What the hell just happened?" Gina was pacing and Scott looked as though he would pass out at any second.

"You believe us yet?" Macy's voice was thick with anger as she buried her face against Collin's chest.

Moth pulled off his shirt and tied it around Kane's leg; While Scott took his shirt off to place over Cassie's face.

Veda came over and helped Cliff to his feet, leading him to sit with her on the stairs.

Kane stood, trying to get the picture of what had just happened out of her head.

Gina stood in front of her, "Get us out of here."

"That's what I'm trying to do, Gina."

Gina grabbed her arm, "We'll do a better job at it."

Kane pushed Gina away as she went to the walls again, studying them, she was sure she would find the way out.

'Out.'

Kane looked up, struggling to see where the exit was.

'Things are not always as they seem.'

Kane frowned as she replayed the words over and over in her mind.

"We're going to die," Layla slumped against a wall, "You've put us in an airtight room with nothing but walls."

Kane spun, "That's it! The exit is in the wall somewhere." She started hitting one of the walls with the crowbar.

The others caught on quickly and Brent, Kelso and Moth also started hitting at the walls.

No one could have noticed Zack edging closer to Layla.

"I've got it!" Brent had found the opening as he broke through the wall, revealing a small tunnel.

Kane collapsed against the wall; relieved that it was finally over.

Moth ran over, kissing her, "We made it."

"Not so fast."

They all turned to where Zack stood behind Layla with his hands around her throat.

Kane stood, "Zack, what the hell are you doing?"

He gave her a small, sadistic smile, "You see, Kane, your boy Goran is here and he misses you terribly, and he hired me to make sure he gets to see you again, so I'm afraid, I can't just let you walk out of here."

Kane didn't take her eyes from Zack, "Brent, start getting everyone out."

Zack frowned.

Kane took a step forward, "It's me he wants; not them. Let them go, and I'll come with you to Goran."

She briefly heard Cliff arguing with Kelso and not wanting to leave.

"Zack let Layla go."

He laughed, his eyes flashing with cruelty before he snapped her neck and dropped her body to the floor like it was dirt.

Moth stepped in front of her, "Kelso, make sure London gets out."

Kane pulled her arm from Kelso's grip, "What? No! Moth, no."

Moth turned to her, "Do this for me, and I promise I will see you out there."

Kelso pushed her into the tunnel and followed behind her.

She fell out onto damp grass; the sky was dark and a light rain fell, and she had never been happier to be outside.

Getting to her feet she joined the others.

Kelso came to them, "Get moving."

They hadn't gone far when Kane turned back to see a large mass of spirits coming towards them, "Guys, you might want to start running."

The others did, taking off at full speed while Kane hung back before turning and running back towards the asylum; she ran through the crowd of spirits as fast as she could.

She had seen the flames on the far side of the asylum.

Crawling quickly through the tunnel, she fell into the water which was now red from Zack's blood; his body lay face down.

Getting to her feet, she saw the basement door open.

Then it hit her; Moth knew that Goran was in the building, obviously, he wouldn't just come out.

He was going after him.

She ran up the stairs, taking two at a time, pausing when she reached the top to figure out if she should go left or right.

She went left, considering that had been the way they had come from.

"Moth!" She knew that calling to Moth wasn't the best idea because she would possibly alert Goran.

However, finding Moth was worth the risk.

"Moth!"

"Kane." A sick sadist voice called over the speakers in a blood-chilling sing-song voice.

Goran.

"I have your flame thrower, Kane."

Kane spun frantically searching as if she would be able to see him from the corridor she was in.

"So, my dear, Kane, I will be waiting for you, unless you want me to continue playing games with this pathetic waste of skin," he paused long enough for her to hear a punch followed by a muffled grunt, "And he doesn't even like his flames." He laughed and she heard the lighter click on and more muffled groans of pain.

"Goran! I swear I am going to kill you."

"Kane, hurry and find me before I peel his skin from his body. And before the building burns down thanks to him."

Kane felt like she was going crazy as fear for Moth set in and she tried to figure out how she would find them in time.

She screamed, punching the wall and hearing bones crunch; the adrenaline of the situation kept her from feeling the pain.

'Experiments lab.'

Kane jumped as the pendant went hot as she heard the female voice once again.

She had no knowledge of where she was going but her legs moved on their own accord.

She stopped in front of a room that held machinery scattered around it.

And there, in the middle of the room sat Moth tied to a chair.

Kane crawled into the room, hiding behind one of the machines; getting as close to Moth as she could without Goran seeing her.

Her heart ached when she saw Moth; the side of his face was bruised with a trickle of blood running down it.

And then she saw Goran; he walked up to Moth and smiled, "She'll be here soon."

Moth spat at him, "She's not stupid enough to come to you."

Goran laughed, "Oh, but she is when you're involved; that woman is loyal down to the last fiber in her body."

"You're wasting your time; she isn't even in the building."

Goran smiled, "We'll see," he went over and pressed the button before speaking into the speaker, "We're in the lab, dear, not far from the second dining hall."

Kane glared at him from her hiding place, trying to think of a plan and searching for anything she could use as a weapon against him.

Goran turned back to Moth, "Call for her."

Moth scoffed, "Never." The pain was thick in his voice.

Goran flipped the Zippo open, "I wasn't asking, Moth."

"Go to hell."

Goran leaned forward, the flame against Moth's arm.

Moth's jaw clenched as he fought against the pain.

Kane couldn't take it any longer, "Stop!" she shouted as she jumped to her feet.

Goran closed the Zippo and dropped it, turning as he clapped, "Babe! How nice of you to finally join us."

Kane glanced at Moth, "You okay?"

He turned his head to her and she gasped, his face looked even worse than she had thought.

"London, what the hell are you doing here? You need to run." He winced from pain as he spoke.

Kane turned to Goran, "I'm here; let him go."

Moth struggled in the chair, "London, get out of here."

Kane took a step forward, "Goran, let him go, he has nothing to do with any of this. Unless of course, you want to just stand here and wait for the fire to reach us."

Goran smiled, "I have no problem with that, Kane."

Kane sighed, crossing her arms over her chest, "Goran, what

do you want?”

"What I've always wanted; you in your rightful place with me, where you belong." He took a step towards her, and she didn't move; challenging him.

She briefly noticed that Moth was trying to free his wrists and she knew that she needed to keep Goran busy long enough for Moth to get free.

Kane let out a mocking laugh, "Goran, do you really think that I would ever go back to you? Not even if you paid me, hell, not even if you were the last guy on earth," she shook her head, "Your desperation is sad and pathetic. You are sad and pathetic."

Goran clenched his jaw, "Don't push me, Kane."

Kane laughed again, "Why? You'll become a little more pathetic? I pity you, Goran."

He made an almost growling sound before he charged at her.

His hands went around Kane's neck in an instant, "Don't think that I won't kill you."

Kane laughed, "Don't think I can't fight back now, bitch." She brought up her fist, connecting with his jaw, making him let go of her and stumble back.

She punched him again, this time making contact with his cheekbone.

He shook his head, recovering quickly and sending a punch to her face, forcing her to take a few steps back.

He came at her again and she kicked him at the back of his knee, dropping him to his back.

Kane ran to him and as she went to kick him, he grabbed a hold of her ankle and pulled, sending her down to her back with a loud thud.

He jumped to his knees, punching her in the face once before moving on to her ribs.

Suddenly Moth pulled him off of her, throwing him to the floor; he jumped over him, delivering punch after punch.

Kane could smell the smoke, and Goran was unconscious, "Moth, we have to go."

He got up and went over to her, "London, are you okay?"

She nodded, "I think so, although my ribs and hand are killing me, I'm sure there are a few breaks."

He lifted her in his arms and started towards the exit, "London, why did you come back?"

"I saw the flames and realized you were still in here."

"London, I-"

Kane cut him off, "Let's just get out of here, we can talk later."

Moth sighed, but nodded, kissing her on her forehead before walking down the basement steps.

Kane frowned, he had wanted to tell her something for a while, and she knew it must have been important.

13

Chapter 13

Kane opened her eyes in a hospital room.

It had been three days since they had escaped from the asylum and the next day would be the combined memorial service for the five who hadn't made it.

Kane closed her eyes and had her own moment of silence for them; Jack, Layla, Mac and Stacey.

And poor Cassie.

Cliff had been to see Kane every day and Moth was almost permanently with her, even when she hadn't been awake.

Gina and Scott were still staying with Alice for a few more days before they planned to leave.

The door opened and Kane was surprised to see Rick.

"Hey, Kane, how are you feeling?"

Kane frowned, "I guess I'm fine."

He sat down on the edge of the bed, "Sorry, that was a stupid question."

Kane nodded.

"There were six bodies found in the asylum."

Kane's head snapped up, "Six? That can't be right. Goran was in there too."

Rick nodded, "I know; we've sent the remains to the lab."

Kane ran a hand through her hair and let out a shaky breath.

Rick surprised her by leaning forward and taking her hand, "Kane-"

The door opened and Moth walked in, "Am I interrupting something?"

Rick let go of Kane's hand and stood.

Kane shook her head, "No, Rick was here to tell me that the bodies are going to the lab."

Moth nodded, "Right," he turned to Kane, "you feeling okay?"

"A bit better; my leg is killing me, but the broken ribs and knuckles I can deal with." Her knuckles were broken and Goran had left her with four broken ribs.

The burnt patch on her thigh that Screaming Sally had left was the worst of her injuries; it was charred looking and kept oozing.

"I'll see you around, Kane." Rick walked out quickly.

Moth took a seat on the edge of the bed, "I still don't like that guy; first he hates you then he's visiting you in hospital."

Kane rolled her eyes, "Moth, come on."

Moth sighed and took her hand, "London, I still need to talk to you."

"About what?" Even as she asked, she had a sinking feeling in the pit of her stomach.

"I don't want to have any lies or secrets between us," he looked up from their entwined hands, "London, Rick was right; I did cut the brakes on Alice's car, I did it because she hit you and I went crazy; I couldn't stand that she had hurt you."

Kane's blood ran cold, "You could have killed her!"

"Keep your voice down," he squeezed her hand, "I'm sorry, I know I shouldn't have done it, but she was treating you so badly and I just couldn't take it."

'The curse.'

Kane frowned, "Moth... You said your dad deserved to die in that fire on Misty Hill... does that mean?"

Moth looked at her and she could see the answer in his eyes even before he spoke, "London, he needed to be stopped. I didn't know that all those people would get hurt, he was supposed to be alone, and I didn't know Willow would be there... she's the one who's been haunting you in your bathroom."

Kane was in shock, she hadn't expected any of that, and her heart ached at the thought of Moth being capable of all of those terrible things.

"London, please, don't look at me like that; please don't look at me like everyone else. I've changed since meeting you; I'm not the same person I was when I set that fire."

Kane pulled her hand from his, "You need to leave."

"London, please."

Kane shook her head, "Moth, don't even try it; I stood by you the whole time, and you've been guilty, you've been lying to me."

Moth stood and started pacing, "Because I didn't want to lose you; don't you remember how I tried to keep you away from me? I never wanted any of this; I didn't want to fall in love with you because I knew I would lose you."

Kane cleared her throat, "Moth, please, just go."

"London, I love you."

Kane turned away so she wouldn't have to see the heartache in his eyes, "If you don't leave, I will have security remove you."

He stood still for a few seconds before walking out and closing the door behind him.

When he was gone, she allowed the tears to fall.

The door opened a few minutes later and Cliff, Collin and Macy walked in.

Cliff was at her side immediately, "Kane, what's wrong?"

If it had only been Cliff there, she would have told him, but she knew Macy had never been a big fan of Moth's and she didn't feel like having that conversation with her.

"I'm fine; everything is just hitting me now."

Macy frowned, "Where's Moth?"

Kane shrugged, "He had stuff to do."

Macy frowned, "Oh, I would have thought he would have been glued to your side," she shrugged, "Anyway, Brent said he'll be by later to see you."

Kane nodded, "Okay, can you bring me something to wear for the service tomorrow?"

Macy nodded, "Of course."

Black combat boots hit the ground as Kane got out of the car Kelso had been driving Cliff, Collin and Macy got out of the back.

Macy had brought along a few outfits for Kane; she had gone with a simple black dress with black tights and black combat boots; the tights over the burn on her leg were hurting but she kept her face void of any pain and emotion.

Kane walked up the church steps and into the old building; scanning the pews.

They were filled with friends and family of the lost; Kane could tell who the parents were immediately.

She was reminded of the service for her parents, and as she searched for a place to sit her eyes landed on Moth, who stood at the back of the church, almost going unnoticed.

Kane turned away quickly, taking a seat next to Rick.

Kelso took a seat next to her, and her friends followed.

Kane nodded at Rick as the preacher stepped up and the service began.

The service went by quickly, and when Cliff stood to speak of Cassie, Kane went with him, holding his hand tightly.

After the burial, everyone had gone to Layla's parent's house.

Kane had started feeling a bit too closed in with all the people and walked out to sit on the front steps.

"This is probably the worst place to say it, but you look nice."

Kane looked up, "Rick, I have a bandage on my hand, bruises all over my face, and you think I look nice?"

Rick sat next to her, "You do. So where's Moth?"

Kane looked away, watching the traffic go past, deliberately ignoring his question.

Seeing Moth at the service had been hard enough, the last thing she wanted was to have to speak of him.

Rick cleared his throat, "Kane?"

"He was at the service. But he knows how people feel about him, so I guess he decided to stay out of their way." She replied, hoping that she had sounded bored and un-interested instead of hurt and breaking.

"Kane, I can see something is up."

Kane shrugged, "I just found some things out, is all."

"Like what, that he's guilty?" He laughed, clearly joking.

Kane didn't respond, hoping she wouldn't start crying again.

Rick frowned, "Wait, what? You did find out he's guilty of that fire."

Kane sighed, "Could you not?"

Rick sighed, "Kane, for what it's worth, I'm sorry."

Kane nodded, "Thanks."

Rick put an arm around her shoulders and she lent her head

against him; surprised that it wasn't awkward at all.

"So how's Veda doing?"

Rick shrugged, "I don't know, I saw her with Cliff earlier though."

Kane frowned slightly, "I thought you two guys were together."

"I left her shortly after Brent found out about us."

Kane was about to speak when Moth walked up to the steps, freezing when he saw Kane with Rick; Kane could see the anger flash in his eyes.

'

"London, can we talk, please?"

Kane so badly wanted to say yes and hear him out, but she wasn't ready yet.

He had lied to her before; there was no stopping him from doing it again.

The door opened and Cliff and Kelso walked out.

Kelso frowned, "Where have you been?"

"London, please, we need to talk."

Kane could feel the tears threatening to spill as she spoke, "Moth, you need to go."

Cliff frowned, "Wait, I'm confused, what's going on? I thought you guys were okay?"

"That was before Kane found out he actually did set that fire on Misty Hill."

Kelso glared at Moth as he realized he had told Kane the truth.

Moth turned to Kane, his eyes filled with hurt, "You told him."

Kane jumped to her feet, "No! God, no, Moth, I would never do that, you should know me better, he guessed."

"I thought I did know you better but that was before you started looking at me like everyone else."

Cliff walked down the steps, stopping in front of him, "Moth, you started that fire on the Hill?"

Moth nodded.

"Why?"

Moth sighed, "We all know what my father was, he had to be stopped, I didn't know so many people would be there; I didn't know how many people would end up dead."

"So you lied to Kane?"

"I didn't want to lose her; I still don't want to lose her."

Cliff surprised everyone when his fist connected with Moth's jaw, sending him stumbling back a few steps.

"How dare you hurt her like this and still say you love her?! You don't screw up like that and just expect her to just forgive you. You better work for it and prove you're worthy of her love. And for now; just go, you're upsetting her." Cliff turned and walked up the stairs, ushering Kane back into the house.

Kane was still surprised by Cliff's sudden outburst, "Whoa, since when do you go all Rocky on me?"

"I'm sorry, K, I just hate that he did that to you, especially after you've stood by him as you did."

Kane sighed, "Cliff, he cut Alice's brakes."

"What? Kane, that's still an open investigation, you need to tell Rick," He grabbed her by the waist and tried to pull her towards Rick, "Come on, you need to let Rick know."

Kane shook her head, "No. Cliff, look, what he did was wrong, and I haven't forgiven him, but I won't turn him in."

Cliff looked as if he was contemplating arguing but shook his head and kept his mouth shut instead.

Kelso came up to them, "Kane, can we chat?"

"Sure, I'll see you later, Cliff." She followed Kelso into the kitchen, "Kel, if you're going to tell me I should give Moth a chance…"

Kelso shook his head, "No, I won't do that. I just want you to know exactly what happened; I may not have known you for long, but I care about you."

Kane sighed and crossed her arms over her chest, "He admitted to starting the fire, he also admitted to cutting the brakes on Alice's car."

"Kane, his father was a really bad person, no one could stop him, no one would even try… He killed Moth's mother, the only way Moth could stop him was by killing him, I can't explain how his father was but I completely understand why Moth did what he did, he did what he had to. And the only reason he didn't tell you sooner was that he didn't want this to happen, he didn't want to lose you; he loves you."

Kane sighed and walked out, leaving the house and heading for the lake, she felt completely hurt and lost, and emotionally she felt ready to explode.

Sitting down in front of the lake, she winced from the pain in her thigh and took her boots off before taking off the tights; they had been killing her.

She looked down at the bandage wrapped around her leg, "We'll you're going to leave an interesting scar."

'Talking to yourself again, eh?'

"Get out of my head."

Suddenly the female spirit with the bloodied hole in her chest appeared in front of her, hovering over the stream.

'The curse needs to be lifted.'

Kane frowned, "What?"

'Stay away from him.'

"Who?"

'My son.'

"Who…" Kane's eyes bulged, "Oh God, are you, Jasmine?"

The ghost didn't reply, her eyes went to the chain around Kane's neck.

Kane gasped, "Oh, God, you're Moth's mother."

'You need to break the curse.'

Kane stood, "How?"

Jasmine disappeared without another word.

Kane sighed before putting her boots on and started a slow walk home.

The one thought, out of everything that had happened was the fact that Jasmine Star had told her to stay away from Moth.

It wasn't like she had planned to go running back to Moth instantly, but she had been certain that in time they would fix things and work towards being okay again.

Now with what Jasmine had told her she wasn't sure what she would be doing.

She didn't even know what she wanted to do anymore.

When she got home she opened the door quietly in the hopes that no one would notice her; of course, she had no such luck.

"You're late." Gina stood in the lounge, still in her black shirt with long black pants she had worn to the funeral.

Kane glanced at the clock, "It's five."

"Memorial has finished an hour ago."

Kane raised a brow, "Are you, my parole officer?"

"Where's Moth?"

Kane shrugged and walked into the kitchen, going over to the counter to make herself coffee.

"Kane…"

Kane frowned but didn't turn around, if Gina had something to say, she would say it, no matter the situation, this was an act.

Gina came over to stand next to Kane, leaning against the

counter, "I can see something is wrong; talk to me."

Kane let out a humorless laugh, "Gina, come on, you don't really care. Even if you were the last person on earth, I wouldn't tell you about my problems."

Gina looked outraged, "Kane, are you forgetting that I'm your best friend? Since you've come to this place you seem to forget that. This dump and the freaks in it have changed you."

"No, Gina, you were never truly my friend, coming here just opened my eyes to that," she took her coffee and walked into the lounge, fully aware of the fact that Gina had followed her.

"Kane, it's like there's something wrong with you; like you're a bomb waiting to blow." She sat down across from Kane.

Kane sighed, "Gina, please, I'm not in the mood."

"Kane, I'm actually worried about you."

"Oh please, save your fake worry for someone who's stupid enough to believe you." She took a sip of coffee, silently telling herself to stay calm.

"Am I interrupting something?" Asked Scott as he came in and took a seat next to Gina.

"Nope." Kane was aware of how cold her voice sounded.

She got up and went into her room, closing the door, she sat on her bed and waited; surprised when she was met with silence.

She had expected one of the voices to start, or a ghost to appear.

But there was nothing but silence, and it was a welcome surprise.

14

Chapter 14

"So how are you feeling?"

It was a week after the memorial service and Kane was sitting at the kitchen counter with Alice and Kelso.

Kane took a sip of her coffee and smiled at her grandmother, "I'm fine."

"Happy now that Gina and Scott are gone?" Kelso asked with a smile.

"Definitely."

Kelso shook his head, "That friend of yours sure did have a big mouth."

Alice lifted a forkful of scrambled eggs, "I haven't seen Moth around; where is he?"

Kane clenched her jaw, waiting for Kelso to answer; she hadn't spoken to Moth since the memorial and every time she heard his name, her heart still ached.

She had gotten better at keeping her mind busy, but now with Alice asking about him, it all came rushing back.

Kelso cleared his throat, "Well, he's around, he's just been very busy."

Alice frowned at him before turning her gaze to Kane, who kept her head down, suddenly becoming very interested in the scrambled eggs on her plate.

As if on cue, Kane's phone rang, and she answered immediately; happy for the distraction.

"Hi, it's Cliff."

Kane smiled, "Brace-Face, what's up?"

"We're all meeting up at the new diner in town, Cherries, we were wondering if you would like to join us?"

Kane could hear Macy shouting something about being normal again and Kane smiled, "Sure, I'll be there in about ten minutes."

"Great, see you there."

Kane stood, "I'll see you guys later, Cliff and them want to meet up."

Alice nodded.

Kane was about to invite Kelso, but decided against it, worrying that with him there they would ask about Moth.

She took a slow walk to the diner, trying to ignore all the memories of Moth that seemed to be everywhere.

When she walked in, she gagged in disgust; the place was colored in cheerful colors; the walls were bubble-gum pink and blue with large red cherries painted everywhere; the floor was bright green and the counter a bright yellow.

Kane sat at a booth her friends were in and frowned, "Do they realize which century we're in?"

Macy laughed, "Who cares; it has a fun vibe. Anyway, how are-"

Kane cut her off, "Don't."

Brent cleared his throat, "So, Rick said he was looking for you."

Cliff raised a brow, "I thought you guys hated each other?"

Kane shrugged, "He's actually not so bad."

"Who's not so bad?"

Kane turned to see Rick.

Collin laughed, "You, apparently."

Kane kicked his shin under the table, "Brent says you were looking for me?"

"I just wanted to check up on you and find out how you're doing." He said as he awkwardly glanced around the table.

"I'm okay," she scooted closer to Cliff, "Sit."

Brent frowned at her, clearly not expecting that.

"Thanks." Rick sat, looking just as shocked as Brent had, clearing his throat awkwardly when his hand brushed against Kane's thigh.

Cliff smiled around the table, "So, what are we ordering?"

"Coll and I are getting the couples special; it's basically a sponge cake with chocolate ice-cream and hot fudge, and it has two cherries on it."

Cliff made a gagging sound, "I'll stay away from the sweet stuff."

Rick signaled for the waitress and a woman with short red hair came over, smiling brightly at Rick.

"One couple's special with two chocolate milkshakes." Said Collin.

"Regular lunch and coffee." Only Cliff.

Brent looked up from the menu, "Steak burger with chips and a large cola."

The waitress turned to Rick, "And for you?"

He turned to Kane, "That couple's special sounds rather good, want to share one?"

Kane nodded, "Sure, and I'll have an iced chocolate latte."

She tried to ignore the looks her friends were giving the two of them.

Rick ordered a coffee and the waitress walked away.

Macy leaned forward, "So, the sheriff, hanging out with a bunch of kids."

Rick laughed, "I'm really not that much older than you."

Brent scoffed, "Hence, he was sleeping with my girlfriend."

Rick looked awkwardly around and Brent sighed and looked away.

Kane heard a Harley somewhere in the distance and she turned, her eyes scanning the road for the source.

Rick leaned closer to her, and lowered his voice, "It's not Moth."

Kane turned, surprised he had noticed and he smiled, trying to be comforting.

Suddenly Macy turned to Kane, "Where's Moth?"

And suddenly everyone's attention was back on Kane.

She shrugged, "He's around."

Macy raised a brow, "Are you kidding me? He was basically glued to you, and now he's nowhere to be seen. What's going on?"

Cliff sighed, "Drop it, Mace."

"No, we are your friends, Kane, you can't keep stuff from us unless of course I'm wrong and we're just here to keep you busy until you leave."

Kane sighed, "He's responsible for that fire on Misty Hill, and he," she glanced briefly at Rick before continuing, "And he cut the brakes on Alice's car."

Rick spun, clearly shocked that Moth had confessed to that too.

The table was silent as they all processed what Kane had just told them.

"Kane, I'm so sorry."

Kane shoved Rick and got to her feet, "Just shut up." She turned and walked out.

"Kane, wait!"

Kane ignored Rick and carried on walking.

"Dammit, Kane, stop," he grabbed her by the arm and turned her to face him.

Kane narrowed her eyes, "What now?"

Rick sighed, "Calm down; Macy didn't know, none of us know exactly what you're going through, but we don't want to make it worse."

"Then none of you should keep pushing about Moth."

Rick surprised her by pulling her into a tight hug, "Kane, I am really so sorry you are going through this; I cannot even begin to imagine what you must be feeling. But you need to get your mind of everything, come out with me tonight?"

Kane pulled away and frowned at him, "What?"

"Let's get some dinner. Together."

Kane sighed, "Well, I've got nothing better to do."

Kane sat in the lounge in a black dress and combat boots; with the raw burn on her thigh limited her to dresses and shorts.

Alice had been staring at her in silence for the last five minutes, and Kane was starting to get uncomfortable.

She frowned, "What?"

"Where are you going?"

"I don't actually know; Rick didn't say."

"Rick?" Kelso walked in, leaning against the wall, "You're dating cops now?"

"He's not such a bad guy; and we're just friends, he sees that I'm not coping very well after everything and he wants to help."

Alice stood, "Well, have fun." She walked out obviously sensing that they needed to talk.

Kelso took the seat Alice had just vacated, "Have you spoken to Moth?"

Kane sighed, "No, Kel, I haven't and I'm not going to; What he did was so wrong and I can't just forgive him, no matter how much I'd like to."

"Kane, he loves you."

"He should have thought of that before lying to me."

Kelso opened his mouth but there was a knock at the door and he gave Kane a pleading look.

She stood, "I'll see you later."

Kelso stood, "Don't; if Moth found out, it'll crush him."

Kane walked out, forcing herself to ignore Kelso's words and not think about Moth and how he would feel if he found out she was having dinner with Rick.

She somehow managed to greet Rick, get into the car and keep up a conversation of mindless small talk all the while her mind was on Moth and what he could be doing.

They stopped at a restaurant that had small tables outside.

Rick cleared his throat, "I hope this is okay; I figured you weren't into the uptight restaurants."

Kane nodded and smiled before getting out, "It looks perfect."

"Great," he frowned slightly, "Not the only thing." He had lowered his voice to a point where she had almost not been able to hear him.

Kane took a seat trying her best not to become awkward.

After ordering Rick turned to her with a serious look on his face, "Look, I know this was supposed to make you forget about everything for a bit, but we got the test results back."

Kane froze, "Goran wasn't found."

Rick lent over, his hand covering Kane's, "No, those weren't his remains in there."

She let out a heavy sigh, "I expected this."

"I will find him, Kane."

Kane shrugged, "Let's forget about Goran for now; stress-free, remember?"

He nodded, "Yes, stress-free."

Kane glanced at their hands and they both pulled away quickly.

The waiter brought their food and Rick smiled across at her, "I'm sorry if I made you feel awkward; I'm just happy that we can be friends; considering when you first got to town you hated me and I thought you were nothing but trouble."

Kane raised her brows, "Oh, and now you don't think I'm trouble?"

"No, now I know you're trouble. But to be fair, you make trouble look pretty damn good."

Kane coughed, "Stop trying to flirt with me."

Rick shrugged, "I'm not flirting, I'm telling you that you look good."

"Well thank you, and if you're still trying to take my mind off of everything, you're doing a pretty good job."

"I'm glad to hear that."

The rest of the night they spoke about anything that came to mind, and there was no longer any awkwardness between them.

She got home after one after sitting at a field with Rick, looking at the stars.

The night had gone by nicely and she had been able to forget about Goran and everything that had happened in the asylum.

But she had not been able to forget about Moth, no matter how much she had tried, and now as she lay in bed, she didn't care about anything that had happened.

Only Moth mattered.

It had been two weeks since the memorial; two weeks since Kane had seen Moth and she was starting to get worried.

The past week, she had been seeing Rick every night, and where Alice was happy that she wasn't sitting at home feeling sorry for herself, Kelso was not happy with it.

Nor was Brent who had told Kane she should have been getting to know him better instead of Rick.

Kelso had taken Alice to the hospital for an annual checkup and Kane was sitting in the kitchen in a long-sleeved shirt and shorts as she took the bandage and dressing from her leg, wincing at the disgusting looking goo on the wound.

"That is so gross." As she reached for the bowl of saltwater and dabbed the cloth in it, there was a knock at the door.

Getting up, she hopped over to the door, swinging it open, "What?"

Rick grinned, "Is that how you greet me?"

Kane stepped aside, "Sorry, come in."

He walked in, turning as she closed the door, wincing as he looked at her leg.

Kane nodded, "Yeah, hence the great greeting."

Going back to the kitchen she took a seat to start cleaning and bandaging her leg.

"How's it feeling?" He asked as he stood in front of her.

"Painful," she leaned over for a gauze patch, "Cleaning is the worst."

He took the gauze from her, "Let me." He gently started wrapping the bandage around her leg.

Watching him reminded Kane of the night Moth had tried to help her when she had cut her ankle on the fence; the first time she had been on his bike.

Kane sighed, she missed him.

"There you go; all done." He smiled, resting his hands on Kane's thighs.

She cleared her throat, "Thanks."

"Look, Kane, I don't know what's been going on with me, but you've been on my mind for a while now; and I know you're still confused about everything with Moth, but give me a chance; we can take things slow, you don't even have to date me until you're ready."

Kane was staring at him with a blank face; trying to process what he had just said.

He had gone from hating her to wanting to date her.

Before she could realize what was happening, his lips were against hers.

"What the hell is going on here?"

Kane shoved him away from her as Kelso walked in.

She jumped to her feet, "Kelso-"

"No, Kane, what the hell is going on?"

Rick frowned, "Kelso, this is none of your business."

"Nothing to do with me? Have you lost your mind? You have no right to move in on her! Moth is like a brother to me and he loves Kane that means I care about her, got it? You don't get to come here and try and mess with her head."

"I wasn't messing with her head, Kelso! Moth screwed up and she deserves better than some lying killer."

Kane rolled her eyes, "Both of you need to stop. Kelso, Rick isn't messing with my head; Rick, don't you dare run your mouth about Moth."

Kelso scoffed, "He was kissing you!"

"Kelso, who I kiss, is none of your business." Kane walked out, passing Alice as she went onto the porch and sat on the steps.

Rick sat next to her, "Are you okay?"

"You can't kiss me, Rick."

Rick cleared his throat, "Kane, I like you, I just want you to know that, like I said we can take things slowly, as long as you give me a chance; I'm sorry if I went too far."

Kane sighed, "Rick, please go, I can't do this right now."

Rick nodded, kissing her on the top of her head before leaving.

Alice walked out, "What was all that about?"

Kane shook her head, "Don't ask."

"Kane, don't worry about everyone around you; choose who you want, no matter what." Alice turned and went back inside leaving Kane to think about that.

Kane sighed, she enjoyed Rick's company, but she knew where her heart was, and that was with Moth.

There was no doubt that he was the one she wanted.

She decided she would go to see Moth the next day; going back inside she laid on the couch, watching a series about zombies.

Waking up, Kane realized she was still lying on the couch and her leg was aching, her ribs too.

She went into the kitchen to look for pain pills, once she found them, she took a few and made herself a strong cup of coffee and took it with her to the room, putting it on the small dresser while she looked through the closet.

She pulled out a simple dress, taking her coffee with her to the bathroom, taking a long sip while she ran a tub of water.

She took another gulp of coffee before going back to her room, trading in the dress for a long-sleeved shirt and denim cut-offs.

She went back into the bathroom and got into the bath, closing her eyes and trying to enjoy the water.

Suddenly her eyes snapped open and frowned at the taps; they had switched themselves off.

'Let's play.'

Kane stood and wrapped the towel around her, got out and went to her room to change.

On her way to the kitchen, she heard a smashing sound from the bathroom.

She went into the bathroom to find the cup smashed on the floor.

One of the larger pieces shot up and flew towards Kane's neck at full speed; she ducked, wincing at the pain her ribs caused.

She shook her head and walked out.

She went back to the lounge where she put her boots on before leaving.

As much as her body ached for rest, she was determined to speak to Moth.

They had to sort things out between them, she realized that now; she realized she wouldn't be able to let him go, no matter how mad she was with him.

She took a slow walk up Misty Hill, going into the house she looked around, there was no sign of him, "Moth?"

Desperate to find him and make things right, she decided to go to the mechanic's shop where he had been working.

The whole walk there, she had a growing feeling of dread in her stomach that something was drastically wrong.

By the time she got to the workshop, blood had started to seep through the bandage on her thigh.

Walking in, she saw a middle-aged man in greasy overalls, trying to write something down but instead all he was doing was covering the paper in grease.

She cleared her throat, "Hi, I was wondering if you could help me?"

He looked up, "What you need?"

"I'm looking for Moth, I'm his... uh, I just need to find him."

He put his pen down, "Well, he resigned; boy finally got some sense in his head and left Misty Meadows."

Kane felt like she had just been punched in the stomach.

He frowned, "Are you okay?"

"What do you mean, he left?" She knew what he meant but she didn't want to believe it.

"He left; he's not coming back... Look, I'm taking it you're Kane? I don't know why you're standing here and not with him, you're the only thing he ever talks about."

Kane turned and walked out, not even bothering to stop the tears that were streaming down her cheeks.

She had lost the only thing that had meant anything to her.

15

Sneak Peek at Book Two

This is a sneak peak at the second book, Misty Meadows: The Curse

"Kane; those new CDs need to be moved to the new shelves."

Kane stopped in the middle of the isle of CD's and DVDs and looked at the stack of CD's in her arms, "Ry, my hands are a bit full at the moment."

Ry, the owner of Misty Music, looked up from behind the till "Work faster."

Kane rolled her eyes, "Don't be lazy just because you're the boss."

Ry laughed before getting up and going to the stock room in the back.

The town of Misty Meadows had changed a lot in the year after the asylum; in the year that Kane had not seen Moth.

As soon as Moth had left, the haunting stopped; Kane didn't see or hear another ghost.

Two months after Moth had left, Ry had come to town and

opened the music store; he was Macy's cousin and Kane had started working for him the moment she left school.

Somehow, Misty Meadows had been awarded the rights to host some big race and they had been busy building the racecourse for almost the whole year.

"Boo!"

Kane sighed, "Mace, you're not scary."

Ry came over to them, "Mace, help your cousin out; these CD's need to be unpacked."

Macy shook her head, "Can't do, I need to get back to the hospital soon for my next shift; I just came to steal Kane for a quick lunch."

Ry nodded, "Okay, well, enjoy."

Kane nodded and put the box she had down and followed Macy out.

"Did you hear that hotshot racer is coming to town soon?"

Kane shrugged, "I'm not really interested in some hotshot racer."

Macy grinned, "I haven't seen him, but apparently he's gorgeous."

Kane hit her arm playfully as they walked into Cherries, "Macy, you're a taken woman, stop drooling over some racer."

Cliff jumped up from a booth, waving them over and hugging Kane before they took their seats.

Macy frowned at them, "What are you two doing out of school?"

Kane rolled her eyes at Macy, Macy herself was in nursing school; Cliff helped out at the school and Collin was in medicine.

Kane tuned out their voices as she focused on something on the TV about one of the racers that were coming to Misty Meadows.

There was a black and red car with flame detailing and the racer's name across the screen: Jixen Star.

Kane turned away, the surname reminding her too much of Moth.

Macy grinned, "I'm so excited; this race is going to put Misty Meadows on the map."

Kane scoffed, "We're still going to be the crappy little town no one cares about."

The waitress brought them their usual lunches and drinks.

Macy bit into her bacon, "So, Kane, how about I hook you up with one of the racers?"

Collin laughed, "What for; she has Kelso and Rick."

Kane rolled her eyes and threw a piece of toast at him, "Don't talk rubbish."

"Oh come on, Rick is still trying to get with you, and you hang out so much you might as well make it official, plus we've all seen the chemistry between you and Kelso lately."

Kane rolled her eyes dramatically, "You're gossiping like a high school girl, Coll; I'm just friends with them."

"You just don't want to admit you have feelings for Kelso because he was Moth's best friend."

"Macy!" Hissed Collin.

Macy's eyes widened, "Oh, Kane I'm sorry."

Kane shook her head, "Relax, it's fine."

Her phone rang and she answered quickly, "Kel, what's up?"

"Alice sent me to get dinner, what do you feel like?"

"Just get some veggies and pork."

"Got it, see you later, K."

Kane hung up and frowned at her friends who were all staring at her, "What?"

"Just date one of them already."

Cliff nodded, "For once I agree with Mace."

Kane sighed, "No. I'm happy being single; I don't need the drama of a relationship."

Macy gave her a sad look, "Kane, it's been a year now, don't you think it's time to move on?"

Kane hit the table, "Macy, I don't need a man to move on; in case you haven't noticed I've moved on, I do aren't give a shit about Moth." She stood and walked out.

When she got back to Misty Music, Ry came to her, "You okay?"

Kane nodded, "Yeah, your cousin just pissed me off; going on about Moth again."

Although Ry had never met Moth, he knew the story of him and what had happened.

"Yeah, my cousin does have a big mouth at times, I'm sorry."

"It's okay; I just wish she would stop thinking that I'm hung up on moth."

"She's just looking out for you."

"I know." Kane stopped dead when a guy appeared behind Ry; out of thin air.

"I'm going to go get those other CDs." She turned and walked into the storeroom quickly, "Why am I seeing spirits again?"

The ghost appeared again and she frowned at him, "You're not supposed to be here."

He chuckled, "How can you see me?"

Kane threw her hands in the air, "Your guess is as good as mine."

He frowned, clearly thinking she would have had a different answer.

"But you can see me."

"Yeah, I know. So what's your name?" she asked as she took

some CDs from a box.

"I don't remember."

Kane looked up just as he vanished.

The pendant she still wore burned hot.

"Kane, what's taking so long?"

She jumped and went through to the front.

Ry joined her behind the counter, "What's going on, Kane?"

She shrugged, "I just have this bad feeling in my stomach."

"Want to talk about it?"

"No, I'm probably just worrying for nothing."

Ry nodded.

Kane sighed as he walked away; she wasn't convinced that everything would be fine; in fact, she was sure that things in Misty Meadows were about to get very interesting again, and not in a good way.

She busied herself sorting the shelves for the rest of the day, and closed up five when the place was dead.

On her way home, she had the feeling she was being followed, that didn't stop her from making a detour up Misty Hill to go to the house Moth used to sleep in.

She hadn't been there in five months, and not much had changed.

She walked through the house, noting that the mirror was gone, and when she placed her hand on the wall she felt as if she were on fire.

She jumped back and sighed, "How could you do that, Moth?" she shook her head and walked out, saying goodbye to the memory of Moth for the last time.

She hurried towards home, it had started to get dark, and even though there had been no murders since Moth had left, she and the rest of the town still felt uneasy; hardly ever being out alone at night.

When Kane got home, she found the house empty; Alice had left a note saying she had gone out.

She dished herself a plate of food, ate and after taking a bath she went to bed.

"How is this place still running; you're always dead."

Kane looked up at Rick, "Care to rephrase that?"

He laughed and shook his head, "Sorry. Anyway, I came to find out if you would mind taking a walk around the racecourse with me; I need to check that everything is okay."

Kane nodded, "Sure, why not."

Rick rolled his eyes, "Don't get too excited."

Kane shrugged, "Sorry, I'm just bored with this job, all I do is stare at a counter all day."

"So get a new job."

Kane stared at him blankly, "Right, because Misty Meadows is so huge, it just has jobs on every corner."

"It will be huge after this race."

Kane shook her head, "Like I told Mace, it's going to take a lot more than a race to put this shitty town on the map."

Rick laughed, "No faith in us, hey?"

"None at all."

"So what time will I see you at the course?"

Before Kane could answer the door opened and closed as a blond woman in a short, tight pink dress walked in.

Kane groaned.

"Do you have any soothing yoga sounds?"

Kane shook her head, "Nope."

The woman made a strangled sound, "Why did this terrible town have to be picked."

Rick frowned, "Who are you?"

The woman gasped, "I am Vladilena Krasinski. The world's most famous underwear model."

Kane clicked her fingers, "Russian, that's the accent."

"You cannot tell me that you people do not know who I am."

Kane shrugged, "You're clearly not as famous as you thought."

"I am one of the highest-paid models; I've been voted the hottest underwear and swimwear model for three years in a row."

Kane blinked at her.

The woman turned and walked out.

"I don't like her."

Rick grinned, "I could never have guessed."

"Anyway, I'll meet you at lunchtime."

Rick smiled and walked out and Kane picked up the pamphlet for the race; she knew that some of the racers were in town as the first race was set to happen in five days time, and she couldn't help what had entered Misty Meadows along with them.

She sighed and got up to busy herself as she started thinking of Moth, and she couldn't have that or she would start missing him again.

At lunchtime, she met with Rick at the racecourse and was surprised to see how good it looked.

Rick motioned to the photographers, "They're starting photo shoots with the racers tomorrow; we were hoping you could keep an eye on things, like a manager."

Kane frowned, "Why me?"

"Because I put in a good word for you with my brother."

Kane's eyes widened, "Brent's dad owns the track?"

Rick nodded.

"Wow, I had no idea."

"Be here tomorrow morning."

Kane grinned; she knew Ry wouldn't have a problem with it seeing as how dead the music shop was.

Kane stood at the track with Macy as they watched the photographers who were taking pictures of one of the racers; Pierre Jouvert, he was from France with long blond hair tied back in a sleek ponytail, his hazel eyes shining as he smiled into the camera, leaning against his black and yellow Ferrari.

Vladilena stood on one side, while a brunette stood on the other; their skimpy outfits matching the color of his car.

Kane checked her watch, "Okay, enough of Franc, bring in Spain."

Pierre winked as he walked passed and Macy giggled.

Kane crossed her arms as she watched them set up for Mateo Hernandez, the Spanish racer with an impressive black and purple Lamborghini.

"Oh wow."

Kane couldn't help but agree with Macy this time; Mateo was gorgeous, with his long hair left untidy and his rugged look.

The models took their places and were surprised when Mateo caught her eye and smiled at her in the middle of the shoot.

Simply to annoy Vladilena, Kane smiled back.

Suddenly Mateo held up his hands, "Wait, you in the black, come here."

Kane frowned, "What? Why?"

"Your style, it goes perfectly with my car; I want a real girl in my shoots, not these fake girls."

Kane sighed but joined him, watching as Macy did excited little hops behind the photographers.

After the shoot he smiled at her, "I'm new here, would you

give me your number and maybe you can show me the town?"

Kane nodded, "Sure." She had to listen carefully to understand him through his thick accent.

She gave him her number and went over to Macy who was squealing.

"Oh my God! You just gave a famous racer your number!"

Kane went through her checklist to make sure they had done everything that needed doing that day; they had only scheduled two shoots per day.

The photographers took a picture of them for the behind the scenes bit of the article and Macy did another hop, "This is so awesome."

"Miss London?"

Kane frowned at the small, green-haired man who stood in front of her, "Yes. Who are you?"

"Fabio; Vladilena's manager; I couldn't help but notice you in those shoots, and I love you your hair!"

Kane frowned; she had died her long hair a violet color.

"Anyway, I would like to offer you a modeling position with us."

"No." Kane grabbed hold of Macy and dragged her away.

"Oh my god, this race is going to make you famous!"

Kane scoffed, "God, I hope not."

It was ten a.m. and Kane was on her fifth cup of coffee; she had been at the track since five a.m, only getting about two hours sleep after going through all the paperwork.

Macy had a shift, so Cliff and Kelso were joining her for the day.

Alberto Abbiati was late, so they were taking pictures of Ludvik Boven and his blue and white Buggati.

One of the photographers came to Kane, "Where is that damn

Italian?"

Kane shrugged, 'No clue; apparently, racers are divas."

Kelso waited for him to walk away before speaking, "How about we go out tonight?"

"Not tonight, Kel."

Just then her phone chimed with a message from Mateo telling her she looked nice.

She looked up and smiled at him as he came over.

"Mateo, these are two of my friends, Cliff and Kelso, guys this is-"

Cliff cut her off, "Mateo Hernandez, one of the best racers there is; Wow, Kane, you have famous friends."

Kelso made a face.

Mateo touched her arm lightly, "Well, here's to hoping she hasn't got a famous boyfriend yet."

Just then Alberto arrived with his maroon SSc Ultimate.

Cliff had to leave after a few hours and so did Kelso.

Mateo was helping Kane make sure all the fliers were in place.

They had just brought in four boxes of T-shirts for the staff when the phone rang.

"Misty Meadows race track, Kane speaking."

"Hi, this is Deacon Adams, I'm one of the racers, could I speak to someone in charge?"

"I'm in charge, what's the problem?"

"I was wondering if you could move my photo shoot to another day."

"No, I can't."

Deacon started on a rant and Kane hung up on him, telling Mateo what he had said, just s Vladilena walked in.

"Kane, when will my boyfriend arrive?"

Kane shrugged, "Who is your boyfriend."

"Jixen Star."

Kane's heart jumped at the surname, her mind going to Moth.

She sighed and checked her list, "He will get here at the end of the week."

"Great, and don't think you can do what you did with Mateo; Jixen is mine." She smiled before walking out.

Mateo raised his brows, "Well, isn't she friendly."

Kane sighed as Macy walked in and she introduced the two while Macy grinned before turning to Kane, "Your cell is off."

Kane checked to see her battery was dead, "I better get home before Alice starts to worry; you're still coming for dinner?"

Macy nodded, "Of course."

Mateo scratched the back of his neck, "Kane, I was actually hoping to take you out tonight."

Kane shrugged, "Well you can always join us."

Mateo nodded, "That will be great."

The three of them left and for once Kane was happy that Macy didn't shut up, because her mind was elsewhere as they walked; she felt as if someone was watching her.

When they got to Alice's, she was ecstatic to have Mateo; Kelso not so much.

They had been at the table for ten minutes when Kane looked up and in the fridge saw the charred girl, Willow's reflection staring back at her.

Kane jumped to her feet, "Sorry, I don't feel well, I'm going to sleep. Sorry."

She all but ran to her room and closed herself in.

Her phone chimed and she jumped; her phone was dead.

With shaking hands, she clutched the phone and read the new text.

WHAT IS MINE, IS MINE ALONE

Kane dropped the phone; the message was from an unknown number.

But there was only one person who came to mind; Goran Owens.

"I should have made sure he died in that asylum."

Kane had managed to fall asleep at four o'clock which meant by the time she woke up at twelve she was late, and she was the one with the keys to let everyone in.

When she got there the photographers complained and Malcolm Cooper, the Australian with a green 9FFT GT had told her how unprofessional she was.

Kane stood glaring at everyone as the shoot took place.

Next to her someone cleared their throat, causing her to jump.

A tall man with pale skin, green eyes and dark air smiled back at her, "Are you, Kane?"

She nodded, judging by his English accent, he was Deacon Adams.

He handed her a coffee, "I'm Deacon. The coffee is to make up for how I acted yesterday on the phone."

Kane took a gulp of coffee, "You gave me coffee, we're good."

"Great, I'll see you later; I'm going to get ready for the shoot."

Kane nodded, he wasn't too bad looking, and she briefly wondered if Macy was on to something about getting a famous boyfriend.

Her phone chimed and she checked the message;

THAT SMILE SHOULD ONLY BE FOR ME

Kane sighed and put her phone away.

As she watched Deacon's shoot, her mind went to Goran and how to flush him out; she wasn't prepared to play his game of cat and mouse again.

After the shoot, she tidied up and went to Cherries for dinner with her friends.

She sat at the booth where her friends were, "Sorry I'm late, the track was hectic today."

"Who was there today?"

"Malcolm Cooper and Deacon Adams; the Australian and the Brit."

"Sounds fun, was Mateo there?"

"No, but Deacon brought me coffee."

"Hey, there's Rick," Cliff waved and Rick came over and sat down.

"Hey. How are you enjoying the track, K?"

"It's going well; although it would go better without Vladilena."

Collin lent forward, "The Russian supermodel?"

Macy raised a brow, "And how do you know that?"

"She's famous."

Rick shrugged, "I've never heard of her."

Collin glared at Rick, "Thanks."

Macy turned to Kane, "Anyway, I think you should be in more shoots."

Rick turned, "More shoots?'

Kane waved a hand, "Mateo had me in his shoot."

"That's actually a great idea."

"I'm barely getting through the day as it is," she took a sip of Cliff's coffee; "I don't want to add more to my plate."

Kane had left after an hour of being at Cherries; too tired for anything, she ran a bath and lent her head back as she enjoyed the hot water.

The tap began to drip.

"Not again." She sat up and stared at the tap; half expecting it to drip blood.

The tap stopped dripping.

With a sigh, she set her head back again.

Her body ached and she felt exhausted; she could feel herself slipping into sleep.

Suddenly a cold, wet hand wrapped around her neck.

Gasping, Kane jumped up, expecting to see a spirit, but she was met with nothing.

Sighing, she got out of the bath, wrapping the towel around her; she noticed the hand print scar on her thigh from Screaming Sally.

Shaking her head she turned, seeing the writing on the mirror for the first time; HANDS OFF

Kane frowned, "Hands off what?"

She went forward, about to touch the mirror, but before she could, the mirror exploded, causing her to dive back with a yelp.

"Kane, are you okay?"

Kane glanced back at the mirror, but it was intact as if nothing had happened.

"Yeah, Kelso, I'm fine; saw a spider." She stared at the mirror for a total of five minutes before getting dressed and going to her room; after what had just happened in the bathroom, she didn't feel safe enough to close her door.

She sat on her bed and stared at the doorway, jumping as her phone pinged, indicating she had a text;

A SMILE LOOKS MUCH BETTER THAN A FROWN

Kane looked around her room; who could have possibly seen she had been frowning?

Her curtains were closed.

He's back

Kane went cold as the pendant Moth had given her burned hot against her skin.

The ghost from a year ago appeared in front of her; the ghost of Moth's mother Jasmine.

The curse is back you must stay away

About the Author

You can connect with me on:
- http://authorsamanthaomaker.wordpress.com
- https://www.facebook.com/groups/316932646870975
- https://medium.com/@samanthaomakerjacobs

Also by Samantha Jacobs

I have a few books available on reading platforms that are ongoing works.

I also have a number of books that will be coming out available on paperback in the following year.

If you would like to stay informed about my works, please keep up with me on social media.

Captive Affair

https://www.goodnovel.com/book/ Captive-Affair_31000454338

Kinley is an unsuspecting bar lady who is suddenly thrown into a world of violence when she is kidnapped by a dangerous Mafia boss whom her cousin owes money.

He swears to hold her until he is paid in full, but somewhere along the line he falls in love with her.

Will he be able to make her love him back, or will she teach him a thing or two about true love?